THE MAGICIAN'S WIFE

THE MAGICIAN'S WIFE

James M. Cain

Carnegie-Mellon University Press

Pittsburgh 1986

The publisher wishes to thank Betty Ann Stroup, Librarian, Mt. Lebanon Public Library, Mt. Lebanon, Pennsylvania, for her assistance in the publication of this edition.

Library of Congress Catalog Card Number 85-70428
ISBN 0-88748-018-7
Printed and bound in the United States of America

Published by
Carnegie-Mellon University Press
P.O. Box 21
Schenley Park
Pittsburgh, Pennsylvania 15213

Distributed by Harper and Row

THE MAGICIAN'S WIFE

1

Around noon of a bright spring day, on Bay Street in Channel City, Maryland, a man strode toward a restaurant as though he owned it and everything in it. It was a friendly-looking place, of brick painted white, in the quasi-colonial style that bends a knee toward elegance while retaining the common touch, like the bubbles in Welk champagne. Its name, from its columned entrance, was The Portico, and this was also the name of its twenty-two replicas, forming a chain, in Maryland, Delaware, and Virginia. But if the place was somewhat folksy, the man wasn't folksy at all. In every outward aspect he was definitely of that aggressive American breed, the business executive. He was tall, lanky, and gracefully formed, if a bit thick in the shoulders and heavy as to chin, with blue, somewhat expressionless eyes. He wore gray slacks, lounge coat in subdued gray checks, blue shirt, garnet tie, and brown shoes, rather dark. His blond hair, which glinted in the sunlight, may have been the reason he wore no hat. All in all, he had his share of good looks and was certainly not unaware of it as he crunched up the gravel walk that led from the parking lot. But, allowing for strut, the habit of masterful posing, the manner of command, he looked purposeful, as though he had more on his mind than himself, the histrionics of his kind, or lunch.

He skipped onto the portico and pushed through the front

door, finding himself in a foyer with a counter at one side, a cashier's desk at the other, and a dining room beyond, fenced off by a rail with a gate in it. He strode to the rail, nodding to the cashier as he passed, and stood a few moments scanning the dining room for someone to come and seat him. Several girls were nearby, but his eye lingered on one a few feet away, who stood with a knot of waitresses, apparently giving them instructions of some kind. She was indeed something to see, her small, trim figure nicely set off by her dark blue hostess uniform, her skin strawberry and cream, her hair dark, her eyes black and very large. In a moment, at one of the waitresses' gestures, she looked up and saw the man. Coming over, she opened the gate with more poise than most Portico girls have, smiled, and led him to a table—a pleasant one, next to the big picture window. His eyes continued to follow her as she stepped toward another hostess, took a menu from her, brought it and handed it to him. He thanked her, then suddenly blurted out: "I know most of the girls here, but I don't seem to place you, and if I'd seen you, I think I'd remember you. In fact, I'm sure of it. Are you new?"

"Not really," she told him. "I've been with the chain some time, but I move from place to place—though of course wherever I am I help out on the floor. I'm the so-called charm school that Portico has. I'm kind of a den mother to the girls. I teach them how to walk, how to talk, how not to walk, and most importantly, how not to talk."

"Oh—and how they love you, I bet."

He was ironical, but she assured him: "They didn't at first until they saw how my system helps with the problem customer, and began thinking things over. Don't worry, they like me fine."

"Meaning the stingy customer?"

"He could very well be the one."

"And how *do* you handle him?"

"Oh—get his name, for one thing."

"Oh, yeah! Making him feel—?"

"Big. Loved. And—what have you."

"Liberal as to tips?"

"The girls think it helps."

"Of course," he said gravely, "this doesn't really concern me, but just to string things out, keep you there pressing your stomach against that chair—a very cute stomach, that I have to say—suppose he won't *say* what his name is."

"*Say?*" she exclaimed. "You think we'd *ask* him?"

"Well—it's one way to find out."

"Perhaps," she conceded, "but definitely unsmart. Why, it would take all the fun out. He wouldn't feel big any more. The whole point is that when he's called by name, he feels he's so important that people *know* what it is. Why, I'm surprised at you."

She was the least bit flirty and made no move to go. "Then," he asked, "how *do* you get his name?"

"In—various ways."

"O.K., I'm the guy known as tight. I'll hold the stop watch on you—let's see you get my name. I'll time you how long you take."

"Perhaps I already have, Mr. Lockwood."

His astonished stare delighted her, so she smiled, and her round, pretty face showed unmistakable guile. "Surprised?" she asked.

"I'm utterly baffled."

He wanted to know how she did it, in view of the fact that "you haven't been out of my sight since I came in this place," but all she would tell him was: "Where there's a will, there's a how." Suddenly he asked: "So O.K., what's *your* name?"

"Sally."

"Come on, give. Sally what?"

"Why—Sally Alexis, if it matters."

[3

"I—think I'm falling for Sally Alexis."

"What are you going to have?"

She motioned to the menu, bringing him back to everyday things. He opened it, studied it briefly, and said: "I'll have the corned beef, cabbage, and spud."

"It's very good," she assured him, "a new dish they just put out today—but already we're getting reports, quite favorable. I'll have the girl put in your order."

"You'll do nothing of the kind."

That was Mr. Bill Jackson, the manager, who strode up as she turned away, stopped her, spun her around, and held her. "Sally," he went on, "you're serving this order yourself, and then you're standing by—to take notes for one of your neat reports. This is Mr. Clay Lockwood, of Grant's, which sold us the corned beef, and he's here to check on it for them—and perhaps make some suggestions for *us*. You write down what he says. Until he goes, you have no other duties."

She stared at Clay, then headed for the kitchen.

"O.K.," said Mr. Jackson, slipping into the other chair, "I'll be the one to say it: Clay, you've got a hit. It's the biggest thing we've had since we put in the deep-fry crab cakes two years ago next month—but bigger, really, because they're a hot-weather dish, where this is all the year round. And why is it going so big? Because it's handled the way *you* said, without some front-office genius getting in it, with the one idea to louse it. We're doing it your way, so when they do come up with it, what it takes to mess it up, don't say I didn't give you credit."

"Bill, this is nice to hear."

He seemed greatly moved and began reciting the snags the dish had involved, Mr. Jackson interrupting: "Boy, you don't have to tell me."

"Could I have a look in the kitchen, to see how they're doing it there?"

4]

"We'll both have a look, Clay."

Threading their way between the tables, past guests having lunch, they passed through a swing door marked IN and entered a shiny, maple-and-metal kitchen. It had a counter down the middle, on one side of which were a chef, checker, cooks, and dishwashers, and on the other a line of girls, Sally standing with them, waiting for their orders. But things seemed to be stalled, with tension in the air, and Clay spotted the reason. Holding his watch on a pan of boiling water, with six to eight packets in it that looked like legal-size envelopes made of aluminum foil, he suddenly addressed the chef. "Earl, what's the big idea," he asked, "holding things up this way? Your instructions say one minute—they're printed right on the package. I've been standing here two, and there's no good reason for it. It's a warm-up, that's all. This meat is precooked—it's ready except for heating. You don't have to boil it this way."

"Take it up!" ordered Mr. Jackson.

Earl grudgingly nodded at a cook, who speared a half cabbage from a warming pan and slid it onto a plate. Then he speared one of the aluminum-foil packets and eased it onto the cabbage. Then with his fork he teased open the foil, flipping it into a trash can and leaving three slices of corned beef already arranged on the cabbage. With a spoon he added a boiled potato and set the plate on the counter, a polychrome creation, in a previous era perfect for a still life, in this one for a pink, green, and white color photo. Sally scooped it up and darted off through a door marked OUT. Bill, in a few moments, led the way to the dining room, then whispered to Clay: "Wouldn't you know it? There I was, worrying yet about that genius at lousing things, and giving the front office credit for having him in the bull pen, when all the time he was right in my own kitchen. Can you beat that? Well, Clay, can you?"

"He had to be somewhere, din't he?"

[5

"Boy, you can say that again. Be back."

Mr. Jackson, at a wigwag from a girl, darted off, breaking off the conversation as all conversations with managers break off. Clay went back to his table and ceremoniously ate the corned beef, while Sally girl-Fridayed nearby, notebook and gold pencil in hand. He said quite a lot: about mustard sauce, "if, as, and when wanted"; about the potato, "which should dry in hot metal once the water's poured off, to meal it up a bit and take the sogginess out"; about cooking time, "which Earl now understands, but should be stressed in your memo, so other chefs get the point and don't double the work without any good reason." Then, almost without a break, he asked: "Well, how did you get my name? I bite. I want to know."

"Oh, it was simple enough," she answered amiably. "Another thing I insist on with these girls is that they help each other out instead of playing a lone hand, as most of them tend to do if left to themselves. So, when that hostess gave me your menu she also whispered your name."

"Oh, so *that* was it."

"You disappointed there wasn't more to it?"

"No, I admire it. So, that clears it up."

"Doesn't clear *you* up, though. You might have said, while we were on the subject, that you were *the* Mr. Lockwood, Grant's Mr. Big, that I'd heard so much about."

"That would have made a difference?"

"Well? Shouldn't it?"

"I want to be loved for myself alone."

"I'll—take it under advisement."

He began getting outrageous, reverting to her stomach, which once more was pressed to the opposite chair, and calling it "a dream stomach, curvaceous, shapely, and soft." Then he asked: "Did you know your navel shows through?"

"Well, why wouldn't it? It's there."

She didn't move, but sounded a little sharp, and pinked

up. Suddenly he said: "Sally, I've fallen for you, which I suppose is why I say things like that. So why don't we step out? Why don't we do it tonight? At the Chinquapin-Plaza Blue Room or any place you like?"

"Well—I couldn't. Not tonight."

Something about her manner caused him to look at her hard. Then, peremptorily he asked her: "This Sally Alexis—is she Miss or Mrs.?"

"I'm afraid I have to say Mrs."

"As you could have said in the first place," he said in a moment, his face growing quite red. Then, husking up, he added: "I'm sorry I overstepped."

"Will that be all, sir?"

"All I think of now."

When she had gone he sat in a sulk, his face getting redder and redder. Then he took a five-dollar bill from his wallet and slipped it under his plate. Then he got up and, looking neither to right nor to left, made his way between the tables and through the gate, then turned to follow the rail out. But he felt his sleeve plucked, and when he looked she was there, holding out his five-dollar bill. Coldly she informed him: "I don't accept tips, Mr. Lockwood."

"O.K.—but the girl on the station?"

"I'll see that she gets it, then."

He bowed, then stalked grandly out, pausing on the portico to let his chest expand, then heading for the parking lot. His glow got clouded, however, in an absurd, perhaps not so absurd, way. Passing the picture window, he happened to glance inside, and suddenly black eyes locked on his, glittering oddly through the glass. He tried to look away, couldn't seem to manage it. His feet carried him by, but of his own free will, he never broke out of the stare. His walk became a stumble, as he went on in a state of upset out of all proportion to the pitch of one brief moment.

[7

2

Getting into his big green coupe, he drove from the downtown shopping district, where the restaurant was, through canyons of office buildings to a bridge over the Chinquapin River, and on the other side turned into Tidal Boulevard, or Death Avenue, as it was called, where Grant's, Inc., was located. It was a multilane complex beside the river, of lofts, factories, warehouses, piers, and a railroad track. At a heavy wire fence he pulled up, and when a watchman opened a gate, he drove into an asphalt enclosure to a space marked MR. LOCKWOOD. Leaving the car, he entered a low building of industrial brick, which was arranged inside on the split-level plan, with glassed-in offices topside and cold-storage rooms below. Bounding up a metal stairway, he reached his own office, a rectangular glass fishbowl that commanded the whole floor. Calling Miss Helm, his secretary, a dumpy little woman wearing glasses, he told her to "set up" a meeting, for 3:45, of the three chain-restaurant salesmen, the girls in the packing room, all cutters, and the head bookkeeper. Then, after a glance at his call slips, he put on a black quilted coat for warmth and went down to the main storage room. His first act as he stepped through the heavy steel door was to inhale, deeply and attentively, as "Your nose knows."

It caught nothing now but the clean smell of good meat,

red and white hind- and fore-quarters hanging in rows on hooks fitted to trolleys, which in turn ran on an overhead rail system so complex, with its switches and spurs and sidings, that it made the railroad outside seem simple by comparison. After a solemn exhale, he began his afternoon rounds, spending a minute or so in each small room at one side, where things were being done by a force in quilted coats like the one he had on. First he stopped with two cutters slicing Delmonico steaks, using big curved knives and small spring scales, trimming off fat to make the exact eight ounces, and placing them in piles with paper "dividers" between. Presently he nodded and went on to the next room, where roasts were being cut, weighed, and ticketed with metal pins, and then on to another room, where veal, lamb, and pork were being cut. Then, crossing the main room, he went through a door to a room not quite so cold, where machines were being run, the biggest a hot-dog creator, as large and as exact in precision parts as an IBM computer. It took pink ground meat, fed it into a complex that stuffed it into skins, and changed it into dogs. Then, on a belt, it traveled these to a packaging mechanism. When they were wrapped in loose plastic bundles, the belt traveled these to a heater, where the plastic was neatly shrunk, so the bundles came out tight, falling into a basket and bouncing like playful pups. Finally it traveled them to a labeler, which covered one side with a happy scene of children having a cookout and eating dogs named GRANT'S.

He tarried briefly by this mechanical miracle, but then passed on to a smaller machine, tended by several girls, and gave it close attention. Its main part was a slicer, to which a girl clamped meat, big slabs of beef brisket, already corned, cooked, and chilled. A rotary blade took off big even slices, which dropped to a belt. From it another girl took clutches of three slices each, and placed them on squares of aluminum foil. Other girls folded the foil, crimped it, tucked the shining packets so formed into boxes, and pasted on labels showing a gay restaurant scene and carrying the caption:

ATTENTION, CHEFS!

This Dish Is Ready to Serve!

NO COOKING—NO CARVING—NO WORK

Heat in Cover One Minute—Remove Cover

THAT'S IT!

IT'S READY!

"Kids, you're doing fine," he told the girls. "Looks like we got a smash." The girls, who seemed to like him, twittered their thanks.

He held the meeting in the "file room," a place filled with cabinets, but large enough for the chair Miss Helm brought, and having a desk with phone. At the last moment he remembered Hal Daley, his chief salesman and right-hand man, and invited him himself. He gave Hal the place of honor, at one side of the desk, opposite Miss Helm. Then he stood at the door, waving the others in, the salesmen and cutters, all quiet, well-dressed men; the girls from the corned-beef unit, looking quite collegiate, and much slimmer now that they'd shed their thick coats; and Miss Niemeyer, the chief accountant, a tall woman, with an intellectual face, who habitually held her glasses over one thumb. When all were seated, he took his place at the desk, saying he wanted to bring them down to date "on this corned-beef thing—but first let's call Portico, see what the score is there." But the call to Mr. Granlund, Portico's president, ran into a snag, as Miss Helm cupped the phone and told him: "Nelly says he's not there. Will you call in twenty minutes?" His face darkening, he took the phone and growled: "Nelly? Have Mr. Granlund call *me*. Tell him it's important, and I won't wait twenty minutes! You have him call me *at once!*" When he hung up, applause broke out from the salesmen, themselves fed up, perhaps, with Mr. Granlund and the difficulty of getting him on the line.

Then the phone rang, and he took the call himself. When a man's voice asked, "Clay, what do you mean, cussing out my girl?" he answered curtly:"I didn't cuss her out."

"You did something, the way she's acting."

"All I did was tell her to have you call, but I can damned well cuss you if you keep up this hard-to-get routine! Who do you think you are, De Gaulle?"

To this, Mr. Granlund bellowed: "I'll not have Nelly mistreated—I won't have it, I won't have it, *I won't have it!*" Then, even louder, but not quite so mean, he asked: "What did you call about?"

"The corned beef. How's it doing?"

"Well, how would I know, so soon after———"

"Steve, quit cracking dumb! The same way I know, by getting with it and finding out! But it's O.K. If you don't care how it's doing, I can always switch."

"What do you mean, switch?"

"Switch to Coastal, what do you think?"

Mention of Coastal, Portico's chief competitor, seemed to enrage Mr. Granlund, for he roared: "Clay, that's blackmail, and I damned well won't stand for it—not for one minute, do you hear?" Clay, suddenly sweet, replied: "I guess it is, Steve. I guess it is, at that, and I certainly apologize. Just the same, blackmail or not, another chain of restaurants, that I won't call by name, gets it—and gets it quick—unless you start making sense. Once more, how's my salthorse doing?"

"Why, O.K., of course. It's big."

"Fine. Now we're getting somewhere."

"And where's somewhere, Clay?"

"I want a year's commitment."

"Commitment? What are you talking about?"

"Oh, for God's sake!" exclaimed Clay, and then, bellowing loudly: "Miss Helm, get me Coastal!" Then, "Be seeing you," he told Mr. Granlund, and hung up. But he stayed Miss Helm's hand when she reached for the phone, and waited. Sure enough, it rang, to a big laugh from the meeting. "We were cut off, Clay," said Mr. Granlund when Clay answered. And then: "That commitment—you want it in writing?"

"Stop clowning," said Clay. "Your word's plenty."

"Then we'll make it a year, but give me a week on exact amounts. It's too early yet to be sure how much we can sell. On a daily basis the demand might drop once the novelty wears off."

"Take a month."

"But now, Clay, I want *your* commitment."

"*My* commitment? How so?"

"I must have this thing exclusive."

Caught by surprise, Clay tapped the desk with a pencil, taking a moment to think. Then, parrying: "You mean, in the area?"

"Well, we have no interest elsewhere."

"So let's see, let's see."

"I want no knife in my back from Coastal."

"Then, O.K.—it's yours alone *provided* we get menu credit. This must be *Grant's* corned beef you're selling—Grant's corned beef, cabbage, and spud."

"Well, I thought *that* was understood."

"Then, Steve, we're set."

He hung up to a round of applause, not only from the salesmen but also from everyone in the room, clearly implying pent-up resentments that his triumph had handsomely requited. He nodded, then got up and took a bow, saying "Thankew" like Bob Hope and "How sweet it is" like Jackie Gleason. Then a bit sheepishly: "*So*, our meeting's over before it's started! It's all wrapped up and presold—but thanks for the memory!" They all laughed and he laughed, but once again, as when drinking in Bill Jackson's praise, he betrayed deep emotion in sharp contrast with his temper, so marked with Sally, Portico's Earl, and Mr. Granlund. And yet they seemed somehow related, as though facets of something else, a deep, consuming vanity that on the one hand hated frustration and on the other thirsted for praise, for understanding, for fellow human warmth. In the end, as they all started filing out, he rapped for quiet again, and told them. "I would forget the best news of all! Without my saying a word, he let drop all by himself: *It's to be a daily feature!*"

This got a hand and a cheer.

He sat down, quite overcome for a moment.

Back in his office, he put in a call to Mankato, Minnesota, where the company's main office was, and asked for Pat Grant, the president. Ostensibly he was requesting outsize beef, "the bigger the better—I can sell all you let me have. Big meat is on the way back, and I don't know what looks prettier on the plate than a half-acre slice of roast beef." But then, almost as an afterthought, he mentioned the day's coup and swelled again to Pat's praise. By five he was at the yacht club, playing billiards with Mr. Garrett, one of the habitués. It was a pleasant, rambling place, with a glassed-in balcony running around the second deck, its front facing Chesapeake Bay, its rear the yacht harbor, a pretty jumble of jetties, cruisers, and sailboats on a cove that made in from the river. By six he was at dinner on the bay side of the balcony. By seven he was home at the Marlborough Arms, an apartment house on Spring Street at John F. Kennedy Drive, formerly West Boulevard.

His place, on the seventh floor, was quiet, spacious, and airy, and he was secretly, perhaps not so secretly, proud of it. It had an entrance alcove, with phone table, closet for wraps, and arches that led to the living room on one side and to a long hall on the other, along which were dining room, kitchen, bath, bedroom, second bath, and second bedroom— though this last was fixed up as an "office," with typewriter, filing case, and dictating machine. The kitchen was a miniature World's Fair exhibit, full of twenty-first-century gadgets, which he used on his inspirations, such as the corned beef. Office, bedroom, and dining room were in birch, not very original and not very masculine. But the living room was his, and masculine in every detail. It had large windows, looking down on city, river, and bay. Between windows were shelves filled with "books that I read," mainly on history— handsome sets of Parton, Nevins, Van Doren, Freeman, Sumner, and the Bancrofts. They stopped at eye level, and over them, standing, leaning, or hanging, were all sorts of things: his framed diploma from Lafayette College, cups he once won for swimming, pictures of Grant's conventions, and quite a collection of paintings, line drawings, and woodcuts, mainly Mexican. At one end of the room was a Steinway baby grand, and near it a record cabinet, with spinner, hooked up to a hi-fi system. The furniture was upholstered in crimson, and each chair had a table beside it, holding ashtrays and cigarettes. Facing the windows was a fireplace, a brass basket of wood beside it, a fine-mesh screen in front. Flanking it were two sofas, a cocktail table between. But a rug was the room's most striking feature. It was Persian, very big, and soft to the feet over its waffle-rubber foundation. Its colors were rose, yellow, blue, and gray, but with the gray predominating. It blended subtly with the dusty tone of the paintings and with their weathered raw-oak frames.

"So! You made a sap of yourself, didn't you? Talking about her navel—now, there was an idea for you, something to thrill any girl! And then when she smacked you down you had to blow your top—get sore, like any third-rate jerk, like

some goddam truck driver. Aren't you ever going to learn?
Well, you never have. . . . Forget her! She could have said,
couldn't she? Then it wouldn't have happened! Why the hell
didn't she say? You asked her plain enough, and—knock it
off, will you, forget her! You want to set yourself NUTS?"

He got this off to his mirror, a full-length one set in the
closet door in his bedroom, for, like many who live alone, he
had formed the habit of mumbling while tramping from
room to room—but sometimes went further than this and
had things out with himself directly. He calmed himself
down, however, went into the living room, and without turning the floor lamps on, sat down in a chair by a window and
stared out at the gathering dusk. After some time the phone
rang. "Mr. Lockwood?" asked a girl when he answered.

"Speaking," he said.

"This is Sally Alexis."

"Oh!" he exclaimed, and then again: "Oh!" But his voice
sounded muffled and queer, and she seemed nonplused
when she said: "You—remember me? The girl who served
your lunch?"

"Why, sure I remember you. Why, yes—of course I do.
Over at Portico. Well, what's on your mind?"

3

But he sounded queerer than ever, and moments of silence went by while he cupped the phone with one hand and banged his brow with the other, telling himself, "Snap out of it. What the hell, has the cat got your tongue?" Then her voice cut across his, asking if he *was* Mr. Lockwood. Of Grant's? Mr. Clay Lockwood? Then at last he regained control and was able to speak like himself, with a fair imitation of naturalness. Yes, he told her, he was Clay Lockwood of Grant's, and if he sounded funny, it was probably from force of habit, keeping his voice down, what with people out in the hall—"so as not to be overheard." With apparent relief she said then that that explained it, and then, drawing a deep breath, went on: Well—what I called about—!"

"Yes?" he said. "What did you?"

"Two things, actually. First, your five dollars."

"Please, forget my five dollars."

"Well, I certainly won't. Mr. Lockwood, girls don't acknowledge their tips, and I don't encourage them to—for all sorts of reasons. It just doesn't work out and, besides, could lead to things we'd better not go into. So you won't be hearing from Ida, but I'm not a waitress, so I can tell you that getting a tip like that meant something to her. She has all kinds of trouble at home, and trouble always costs. So her face really lit up when I handed that money over, and I just wanted to let you know."

"Then, O.K.—but please, no more about it."

"So now. So now. So now."

"Yeah?" he said, and then echoed: "So *now?*"

They laughed, a bit breathlessly, both seeming to know that things were about to be said that would mean a lot more than five dollars. She drew an audible breath, then declaimed: "Mr. Lockwood, you did not overstep!"

"Oh, I did. No argument about it at all."

"You did not. I won't have it that way!"

"And—that's the real reason you called?"

"Well, maybe so. It was nice, just the same, that you did leave Ida five dollars, so I had such a pleasant excuse. So all right, it could be the real reason at that—why I looked you up in the book, counted ten—and dialed."

"To say I did not overstep?"

"It wouldn't drop out of my mind."

"I made a pass, though."

"So? Who minds a little pass?"

"I talked about your navel."

"Well, as I told you, it's there."

"I'd love to wobble my finger in it."

"Listen! Are you starting all over again?"

"I'd like to. Why *didn't* you say you were married?"

"Mr. Lockwood, that's the sixty-four-dollar question that I've been asking myself ever since you went out the door. And I'm not sure I know—how do you like that? Now that I have you, at a distance—a safe distance, I mean—on the other end of a phone and can talk in a natural way, be myself, without getting all fussed—I may just as well tell the truth and own up, I didn't *want* to say. I was having a very good time, enjoying it, passes and all. I kept holding it back on purpose, Mr. Lockwood."

"Who's this Mr. Lockwood? To you I'm Clay."

"Then why don't you call me Sally?"

"Sally, where are you calling from?"

"Home. Why?"

"Who else is there?"

"Nobody—I'm alone." And then, getting the point: "Oh, you mean my husband? He's not here, Clay—he works at night. He's in show business. He's a magician. You must have heard of him—he has the act at the Lilac Flamingo. . . . Well, what do you think? That I'd be dumb enough to put in this call to you with somebody listening in?"

"Just asking, that's all."

"Well, certainly *not!*"

"Then—we're back where we were before. Where would you like to go? To step out a little with me? And where do I pick you up?"

"But I couldn't *go* anywhere."

"If not, why not, Sally?"

"I'm too well known, that's why. Clay, I see hundreds of people a day, and a lot of them know who I am. And even if they don't—"

"O.K., visit me here."

"Said the spider to the fly."

"Where do you live? I'll come get you."

"No! No! No!"

She whimpered it like a child, and when he insisted, she hung up to "think things over," saying she'd "call him back." He thought things over too, again in the chair by the window, and thought them over hard. He wasn't a stranger to women, and in the games he had played with them had scored a bit, and most pleasantly. There had been the girl in high school at Trenton, New Jersey, where he was born, and the guilty year with her before they both went off to college. There had been the woman at Easton, Pennsylvania, who had rented him a room his first few weeks as a student, and her liberal ideas about payment. There had been a bank teller at Coatsville, where he had herded cows one summer after getting interested in meat. But the games a student plays aren't really for keeps, and so he had gone his way blithely, with no wounds to mar his memories. Now, however, he would have to play as a pro, and as he looked down at the lights, prickles ran up his back, as though to warn him of danger. When the phone rang, he hesitated. It rang twice before he answered.

If possible, she was even more frightened than he was, or at least seemed to be, and took five minutes on his instructions, "so we don't have any slip-up." She lived on Elm, near Kennedy, just a few blocks away, but the problem was "nosy neighbors," as she put it, so she must leave the house on foot, "dressed as I always am when I go to the picture show—so don't expect any Zsa Zsa Gabor iced up for a personal appearance." She would have to buy a ticket "at the Harlow Theater on Elm Street, from that dumb blonde cashier who lives three doors from me, and be checked by the doorman, who's her husband and doubles as ticket taker." But then "I can slip out the fire door, which is out of sight from the lobby, and if you're parked up the street and wink your lights when I come, I can be in your car in a flash and—you can take it from there. But I *must* be back, must be seen *leaving* the theater, when the late show lets out! Promise you'll get me there! On time!"

He promised, put on the living-room lights, and slipped down to the basement garage, getting his car out again and driving to the theater. He took a turn past it, to be clear on all locations, then drove to a point behind it, parked, and cut his lights. He was surprised at the thump of his heart and not too pleased by it. "Take it easy," he told himself, then repeated it, adding, "goddamit." But he cut off suddenly as he saw her come up Elm Street and turn toward the theater. He stared and stared at the fire door, then thought he saw it move. He winked his lights several times. Then he caught the sound of footsteps, and a shadow moved in front of him.

Then she was tapping on his window, and he jerked the door open for her. She jumped in and he started his motor, putting on his lights and pulling ahead before finding her hand and pressing it. It was cold, and indeed the whole thing had a clammy, underhand feel to it, quite different from what he had expected.

When they reached the Marlborough Arms, he left the car on the street, and they started for the front door. But when he reached out to open it for her she caught his hand and held it. "Clay," she whispered, peering at Doris at her switchboard, "I can't go in there! That girl could know me—I see so many people!" And then, pulling him back toward the car: "Come on! It's a nice evening—we'll take a ride." But he held her and said: "O.K., so you can't go through the lobby. But there's another way—nothing to it." He led her up the alley beside the building to the tradesmen's entrance at the rear, opening it with his key. Then they were in the freight elevator, creaking up to the seventh floor. Then they were tiptoeing along a hall, then stepping through his door. "Welcome to my humble abode!" he said, taking her light spring coat. As he hung it up in the closet she motioned to the rest of her costume, which consisted of sweater, pleated skirt, knee-length black stockings, and loafers. "Did you ever see such a mess?" she asked sourly. "Just ratty-looking, that's all. But that's what it had to be—or else I couldn't come."

It certainly thickened the clammy moment, but he managed to stammer out: "What do you mean, mess? You look fine." She resumed her tirade against the neighbors, but broke off as she turned and saw the living room. Then, almost reverently, she whispered: "I might have known—should have known—you'd live in a place like this." Then, out loud, and bitterly: "*I* live in a dump. Oh, the house is all right—outside, anyway. But inside it's just a storeroom, one endless storeroom for junk: mirrors and mirrors and mirrors; varnish cabinets, with stainless-steel legs; baskets with double sides, baskets with false bottoms, baskets with trick pockets, every kind of basket there is, lined up against the wall, like Ali Baba's jars, so they give you the creeps, and you go around lifting the tops for fear there *are* thieves inside; tables, with servantes, spring pulls, false bottoms—all kinds of different tables; playing cards, feather bouquets, levitation gear, and canopies—they're the worst. Do you have any idea how sick brocade can look, always *pink* brocade, with a silver fringe on it, in the broad light of day?"

"Well, I can kind of imagine."

"I doubt it. Nobody could. You know what it's like, what it's *really* like? Like a Christmas tree in July."

She began inspecting the paintings, then waved her hand at them, saying: "Those things—my mother's an artist—she's buyer for Fisher's and draws their ads for them—those goofy girls that look like the Easter parade—so I know a little about it—*those* things cost you something!"

He told her: "Not really. Those Mexicans paint too much for their work to bring a price. There's a fellow down there who brags that his is the only restaurant in all Mexico City *without* murals by Diego Rivera. But their stuff does have a style, a dry desert smell. Makes me feel in a certain way."

"Me too—like I want to cut my throat."

She sat down at the piano, struck a chord, said: "I love a Steinway—it doesn't sound like any other." She started to play, not well, but accurately, with heavily accented rhythm.

"Chopin?" he asked.

"Mm-hm. Waltz in A flat minor."

"I've heard it. I couldn't have named it."

When she finished, he clapped. "*Je vous remercie, m'sieur,*" she said, getting up.

"Oh? You speak French?"

"It's easy if you lived there; I did when I was little. My father, before he died, was a professor at Goucher College, but he met Mother in Paris when she was an art student there and he was studying at the Sorbonne. They got married there, and I came along quite soon—within the law but without much to spare."

"Your mother sounds delightful."

"She's terrific—young, talented, and beautiful, with a figure to write home about, and I just love her—providing she knows her place and stays in it."

"And just what is her place?"

"Out of my hair, Clay."

She resumed her walking around and, perhaps realizing that things were a bit flat, remarked: "*So!* Now you know all about me, my practically unlimited bag of tricks: I can serve corned beef, cabbage, and spud, bat out a waltz on your Steinway, *parlez-vous* French a little, and fake along about art." She sighed, then added, remembering: "*Oh!* And twirl! Now, there's an accomplishment for you!"

"You mean, like a majorette?"

"That's it, and I was one, at the high school football games in Baltimore, where we lived. I was starred between the halves—what got me in trouble later and led to my plunge into show business."

"With acrobatics, no doubt?"

"Oh, yes, especially *them!*"

She was in the center of the room, and with no more ado, pressed her palms to the floor and cartwheeled over toward him, a flash of whirling skirt, silk panties, and soft, shapely legs. Then she came smartly upright before him—or would have except that a loafer flew off and threw her slightly off balance, so she toppled into his arms. Until then their moment at Portico and the other one over the phone, with little cat's-paws of wantonness darting boldly out, hadn't once returned. But now a tidal wave swept over them as their mouths came together and their hungry fingers dug in. Then, lifting her, he carried her back to the bedroom.

4

Two hours later, stretched out on one of the sofas, her head in his lap, she stared at the fire he had built and amiably answered his questions, about her childhood, her family, her schooling. She told of her years in Paris, of others in Baltimore, when her father had been summoned to teach there; of her attendance at Sarah Mitchell School, where "Bunny Granlund taught deportment before she married Steve." This surprised him, and she admitted that at Portico she was Mrs. Granlund's protégée. She told of her father's death and her mother's lean years, "when she couldn't afford Sarah Mitchell and had to put me in Western High"; of how she had twirled with the band, "and then at one of our shows, I was the cute little thing that got picked to be sawed in half, by a young magician who came and helped us with our production." He said: "O.K.—I can imagine the rest of *that*," but she pursued the subject a little, saying: "He's the Great Alexis, and if you haven't heard of him, you must have heard of the Lilac Flamingo, that club in Baltimore where he works." He said he sold the Flamingo meat, and "Mike Dominick's a pal—at least he thinks he is." They laughed over Mike, and she went on: "Of course Alexis is what he calls himself—it kind of sounds like magic, so he took it. He's really Alec Gorsuch."

"Any relation to Mr. El?"

"Mr. El's his father."

He whistled, for Mr. El, with his auto-accessory stores, was a fabulously rich man. She said: "I don't wonder you're surprised that the son of someone like him would get himself mixed up with magic—but you needn't be. In the first place he's hipped on it, and in the second place he doesn't like junkyards, as he calls his father's outlets. So, *that's that*. So pink brocade still looks——"

"Like Christmas in July?"

"Now you know."

She took his wrist to look at the time, but he assured: "I promised you'd go back on time, and on time you're going to go. . . . If you still want to go, that is."

"If I *want* to go? How do you mean, Clay?"

"If you want to go at all."

"That I'd stay? Here with you? Tonight?"

"Tonight—and the rest of your life."

She sat up, staring, and seemingly baffled. Then: "Well!" she said. "I'm not sure I know what you're getting at, but—Clay, we've only known each other since morning. Afternoon, to be exact, as the luncheon menu was out, and it doesn't come from the printers till twelve. For the rest of my—? Honey, is this a gag?"

"No," he said seriously. "Listen, there is such a thing as knowing the big things in life from the little ones, of being able to tell when you've been hit by a truck. All right, I own up, I have been. But you've been making noises as though it hit you too, so why do you call it a gag? What's stopping you from staying here, tucking away with me, and then as soon as you're ready shoving off for Reno, Tahoe, Vegas, or wherever you want it done? Then we get married, that's all. And go on from there. That's simple, isn't it?"

"Little too simple, Clay."

"How, too simple?"

"In—all kinds of various ways."

"In one way, you're damned right it's simple: You'll be here, then—and not there, warming the hay for a husband, when he gets home from his show."

"Oh, so *that's* it!"

"That among other things."

"It's one thing you don't have to worry about!"

She got up, smoothed her skirt, shook her hair, and declaimed: "When I heard about Busty Buster, that girl he has in his act, and what he was doing with her—I locked my door. Did you hear what I said, Clay? I locked it and locked it for good. It was just before Elly was born and——"

"Elly? Who is he?"

"My little boy, who do you think?"

"You—have a *child?*"

"Well my goodness, Clay, I'm married! Wives do have children, don't they? Elly's three years old, and even before he came, I tell you I locked my door. I——"

"I took you for—twenty-two, three-years old."

"I'm twenty-one, so happens."

"Then—O.K., let's get him too."

"He's at his grandfather's now."

She said Mr. El had sent for the boy, to spend the Easter holidays, and had kept him a few days longer, "and that's why I'm free to traipse over here with you." He said: "Then stay, and when we're ready, go get him and——"

"Stop being the Wild Man from Borneo!"

"Is that what I look like to you?"

"Clay, I hate nutty ideas."

"O.K., but what's nutty about it?"

"Everything."

"Is there any good reason you can't——"

"Yes! Elly, for one thing!"

"So he's hanging us up—and I'll tell you what we'll do. I have an office back there, a spare bedroom, really, with fixtures and stuff in it that we can move out tomorrow, so workmen can come in, paint rabbits on the wall, and make a nursery out of it. Then we'll put in his trundle bed and——"

"Please, please, please!"

She was touched, or seemed to be, and sat down on the opposite sofa, getting a handkerchief out of her bag, wiping her eyes and biting her lip. Then, quietly, she said: "You made me cry, Clay—that you'd feel so friendly to him, my own little boy, means something, I can tell you. But where he sleeps and the pictures he has on the wall aren't what I'm talking about. They're important, but they're not all."

"Yeah? And what's the rest?"

"His full, fair share of a fortune."

"The Gorsuch fortune, you mean?"

"Yes. It's what's been hanging things up."

"Things? You mean, a divorce?"

"That's it. Between me and Alec."

"All right, Sally, I begin to get it now, but make it plain, will you? So I get the picture?"

"We're marking time, that's all."

"On what?"

"A—certain event."

"Do you mean the death of Mr. El?"

"Well, I could never make myself say it, but since you have, that's what we're talking about. Until that event takes place, I dare not make a move, because he could resent it, Clay—and take it out on Elly. As it is now, the will's in Alec's favor, with a trust fund or whatever it is, and of course when he inherits, he can make me a settlement and one for Elly too—though mine I don't care about. I'm making a living now and can take care of myself the rest of my life, I think. But my child I can't disregard."

"So where does that put us, if anywhere?"

"Well? Tonight's been sweet. And tomorrow—"

"We do a retake, on the sneak—?"

"All right, if that's what you think it is."

"Think? We *are* on the sneak, Sally!"

"Clay! I stay—and then what? Do you know?"

"I told you! You go to Reno——"

"And get not one red cent! Of what's due me or due my little boy! If that's not being nutty, I wouldn't know what it is!"

"Hey, wait, not so fast!"

His mind had been at work and by now had somewhat caught up. He asked: "How can you hope for a settlement, if a lump sum's what you mean, when the dough's tied up in a trust fund? They won't unfreeze it for you; it couldn't be done. And if alimony's what you mean, it won't run one day after you're married again. So I'm not with it, Sally, at all. And so far as Elly goes, again, if the will names your husband, your boy can't cut in, except as you get an allowance to bring him up, until your husband dies. So who's nutty now?"

". . . I think it's time to go."

"I guess it is."

"My friend, you're through with that girl. Did you hear what I said, dumbbell? They're marking time, all right—or she is—right foot, left foot, and tearing the leaves off the calendar. Because once the old man goes, the only way that she can cut in is by another blessed event, with funeral lilies yet. And you don't volunteer to knock that husband off— she's nice, but not that nice, oh no. She'll be a Merry Widow, that we know for sure, but not with your help. Do you hear? You're through!"

So he informed his reflection in the mirror, after taking her back to the theater, making her promise to call the next night, and rolling behind her on Elm Street, as she skipped along to a pleasant house and went in. But the next night, when he got in from the club, he found a note on his bureau, from Ellen, his cleaning woman: *Mr. L.: This was under your pilow.* "This" was a tortoise-shell comb with a filigree back. He sniffed it, found it full of her delicate smell. Trying to put it down, not quite being able to, he took it into the living room, held it as he sat by the window again, looking down at the city. When the phone rang he answered briskly, as though things were just as they had been at the parting the night before. He mentioned the comb; she said, "Oh-oh-oh," with a guilty laugh. She mentioned the theater's change of bill, "so I can go there again tonight without its looking funny." He waited as before, across from the parking lot, telling his rear-vision mirror: "*Stop borrowing trouble. Don't jump to conclusions, Lockwood. Maybe she means what you think, maybe not, who knows? Take it as it comes. It's just a few nights anyway before the boy is brought back, and that brings it to an end, a natural, easy end, without you smacking her down. Until then, she's pretty nice.*" The next few nights she decided to eat uptown and come to his place in her car. He gave her a key, and she let herself in the back way, scratching on his door, and being welcomed ecstatically.

The last night he gave her dinner, prepared by himself: Grant's steak, baked potato, peas and onions, salad, and ice cream with brandied cherries, with martinis to start things off, and Château Neuf du Pape. It all impressed her no end, except for the wine, which made her laugh. "It costs a lot, Clay—the only thing in its favor. For the rest, it makes you sleepy, and I didn't come here to sleep." Putting the bottle back without letting him open it, she found a Château Margaux and pulled the cork herself. "Claret's all right," she said. "It's light, it leaves your head clear, and goes fine with steak. That other—it's for the tourists, really." Such Escoffier talk delighted him, and he spent an enchanted evening, listening to tales about Elly, his beauty, his angelic disposition, how he was loved in the day nursery where she put him each morning on going to work.

30]

But later, stretched out once more by the fire, she reverted to the future, the first time she had since he brought the subject up. "You know," she said quietly, taking his hand, "I'm beholden to you for opening my eyes to—everything. The spot that I'm in, Clay. I never realized before what a heads-I-lose-tails-I-can't-win proposition I'm up against. Because that's true, isn't it? That even by marking time I can't get anything or get anything for Elly, can I? If I try for a settlement now, all I can get is alimony, which stops when I marry you, and an allowance for him. And if I wait, it's exactly the same, with Elly nowhere, either, unless Alec should—die. Clay, they talk about four-letter words, but that little three-letter one is the worst in the language for me. It's the truth, though, isn't it? That once the old man—isn't here any more Alec has to—*die*—I must make myself say it—before either one, Elly or I, can—share. Well, as I said, you opened my eyes, and thanks. The next thing is, what now?"

It was some moments before he said: "I've told you what I think. You can't make an omelet without breaking some eggs. Leave him, go to Reno, marry me—and get on with your life. So far as Elly goes, he'll be no worse off. I'm not starving to death, I remind you. I'm plenty able to raise him."

"Clay, that touches me so."

"Will you think it over?"

"I will. I promise. And will *you* think it over?"

" . . . Think *what* over, Sally?"

"There must be some other way!"

"What's wrong with this way? My way?"

"But it seems so awful, Clay! To have my child cut off! Just left out on a limb! With no way to get it—the money that's rightfully his!"

"In due time he can inherit!"

"Yes, but when is that?"

"For that you'll have to ask God."

"You're thinking it over, all right. You have thought it over, and you've come to the end of the plank. You're through—you don't see that girl any more."

5

Next evening, instead of camping by the window, he lit the floor lamps, put on a Tchaikovsky album, and at luxurious ease sat himself down to listen. The *1812*, one of his favorites, was banging briskly along when the phone rang. Smiling icily to himself, he let it go on without answering. *Romeo and Juliet* had started when it rang again, and again he did nothing about it. But twenty minutes later his inside phone rang, and Doris told him: "Lady to see you, sir." Caught by surprise, he hesitated, then said: "Send her up." He cut off the music and stood thinking, trying to fathom why Sally, so frightened of being seen, and having a key of her own to come in the back way, should be showing herself now down in the front lobby. Making nothing of it, he went out in the hall to meet her, closing the door after him and resolving she shouldn't get in, no matter what kind of excuse, what weird, farfetched tale, he would have to come up with. But what stepped from the elevator wasn't Sally at all, but an apparition in black, with crimson hat, gloves, bag, and shoes, that eyed him for a moment and then held out its hand. "Mr. Lockwood?" it asked. "I'm Mrs. Simone, Sally Alexis' mother."

"*Oh!*" he exclaimed after a startled silence. "Yes, Mrs. Simone—Sally has spoken of you. I'm honored."

"To say nothing of flabbergasted?"

[33

"Well, surprised, I admit, but pleasantly."

"I should have phoned, and would have, except I wasn't sure you'd see me, and so, to head off a brush, I barged."

"I'm certainly delighted you did."

"At least it's nice of you to say so."

By now he had got his door open again and ushered her in. Her reaction to the living room was much like Sally's. And while she marched herself around, taking in various things, he stood taking her in, with more of an eye to detail than had been possible out in the hall. He noted the smart hang of the taffeta dress, and the Continental look of the matching stole that was flung over one shoulder after a turn on her neck. He noted the crimson accessories, of the exact shade to bring up her iron-gray hair. He noted the fresh, handsome face, with large hazel eyes. But most of all he noted the "figure to write home about," a slim, sinuous thing of no more than medium size, but voluptuous in every curve. "That dress," he said quickly when she caught him looking at her, "if it was done in dark blue, would be the Portico hostess uniform."

"It's the original of the Portico hostess uniform," she said, a bit tartly. "I designed it myself. And I wasn't too pleased, I can tell you, when Bunny Granlund saw it and thought it was just the thing for the Portico girls to wear. I wasn't too pleased, but it means business to the store—to Fisher's, where I work—and I get a royalty, too, so I don't say too much about it. In the meantime I wear it, *as is.*"

"It's lovely. Simple—and beautiful."

She thanked him and continued her tour of inspection. Then suddenly: "Why this?" she asked. "Why Mexico?"

"Well, why not?" he parried.

"It seems a bit odd somehow. In Maryland."

"It's a long story. I got into meat and then thought I should learn more about it. So I bought a bunch of books, among them one called *The King Ranch*, that I heard really

34]

went into it. It did, all right, but went into other things too, like Texas history, the Mexican War, and that stuff. It cleared up all kinds of things for me, like why they fought that war. Why *we* did was no mystery at all: we just helped ourselves to a strip of desert down there, for no good reason at all except to make a prettier map, and because the Rio Grande was longer than the Nueces and made a nicer-looking boundary. But why would they fight *us?* It was because it just so happened that this strip of worthless desert also included a harbor, the one at Punta Isabella, inside the Brazos Santiago—the only good one they had north of Vera-cruz. No one is quite sure that *we* even knew it was there. So that's why they went to war, and I don't blame them one bit. When I got through with that book, I was hooked on Mexico, and my hat was off to the writer. His name is Tom Lea, and you never heard of him but——"

"I? Never heard of Tom Lea?"

She seemed dumbfounded, and pointing to a drawing of a horse surrounded by cactus, said: "That *is* a Tom Lea—or I'm crazy. Peering close, she added: "Yes—it's signed."

"Oh. He's an artist too—as you are."

"Not in his class—*but I'm working.*"

He said he admired the ads she did for Fisher's, and she seemed pleased, but got back insistently to him. "Why meat?" she wanted to know.

"Well, once again, why not?"

"It doesn't match up, or doesn't seem to anyhow. With these things, this place, or even—you."

"I wanted something big."

"Oh. Now I begin to see."

"Railroads, coal, copper, things like that, which may have been big once, are all washed up now. Power, steel, oil, automation, things like that would have meant more years in college—MIT, some place like *that*. So I happened to think

[35

of meat. It's big and has to get bigger—so long as the population keeps increasing and people have to eat."

"It begins to make sense now, and *is* sort of poetic at that. In a rugged, masculine way. This was before, during, or after Lafayette College?"

"During. But where did you hear about that?"

"You were graduated from there, weren't you?"

"Yes, but I didn't tell Sally."

"Oh, I haven't discussed you with *her.*"

"Then how do you know so much?"

"There's no mystery. Sally, when she goes somewhere at night, has to be reachable, in case something comes up about Elly. And as I'm sure to be called if she doesn't answer her phone, she always leaves me a number—usually Bunny Granlund's or one I'm familiar with. But the other night it was one I didn't know, and when it happened night after night, I got curious about it and called Information. So once I had your name the rest was ridiculously easy—Fisher's credit department did me your bio sketch, of course thinking it routine, and not knowing my personal interest. I know your New Jersey origin, which accounts for that drag on your speech, your very elegant drawl, also your swimming career and your great success at Grant's."

"Nothing scandalous, I hope?"

"No, it's all most impressive."

"Let's talk about you, Mrs. Simone."

He waved her to one of the sofas, then took a seat on the other, facing her. "Meaning," she said, "get to it? What I came about?"

"Well? What did you come about?"

"I'm not sure I'm going to say, Mr. Lockwood. You're—not at all what I expected, and I've been getting the shakes. Talking and talking—postponing as long as I can. I may have been losing my nerve."

"I'll make it easy for you. I think I've guessed why you came, so why don't we—be civilized about it? Go somewhere, have soft crabs on toast or something, maybe wine with bubbles in it—and have our discussion *friendly*."

"I don't understand you at all."

"You came to bust it up, so O.K., start busting."

"To—bust *what* up?"

"What's between me and Sally."

"Then I'm right in suspecting that something *is*?"

"No—that something *has* been, that's all."

She sat staring, trying to guess what he meant without trying to straighten it out by questions that made her seem stupid. He smiled, said: "You're very good-looking. I'd enjoy champagne with you. So, if you're busting it up, then bust."

At last getting the point, she asked: "And you think I'd do that? Try to bust it up by cutting in on my little girl? *Myself*?"

"If you're busting, that's how it's done."

"And you, Mr. Lockwood, after seeing her every night, would now start up with me? I'm her mother—I thought I made that clear."

"Invitation withdrawn. What did you come about?"

"I can say, if permitted."

"I've just been trying to help."

"I'm not busting it up! *I came to egg it on!*"

She closed her eyes as she said it, as though horribly embarrassed, but pronounced every word distinctly, as though she desperately meant it. He was speechless he was so startled, and sat staring. Then he got up, and after marching around, asked: "*Why?*"

"Well, Sally's my daughter, isn't she?"

"Yeah, as you've said quite a few times."

"And—I want her happy. Isn't that enough?"

"Wait a minute. Did Sally ask you to come here?"

"No! No, Mr. Lockwood—she hasn't said one word about you to me! And you mustn't divulge to her that I came here tonight. You'll protect me, won't you?"

"Then, I will. Now, what's the rest?"

"The—rest?"

"*What the hell did you come about?*"

He snapped it impatiently, then plowed on fast, to say what a queer thing it was for a mother to pay such a call, "out of the blue—with no more to go on than a name from Information, a gumshoe job by her store and—that's all. Talk about not matching up, this is just plain queer—unless there's more to it. So there is more to it. So why don't you say, Mrs. Simone?"

"Mr. Lockwood, there's *nothing* more to it!"

"Then O.K., let's have the soft crabs."

"I tell you, I'm Sally's mother."

"And I tell you, Sally and I are through. Maybe you're her mother, but you're good-looking, I like you and—so let's get at the crabs."

"No! No!"

"Why no in that tone of voice?"

"Well, Mr. Lockwood, perhaps I *should* have said more. I haven't quite made myself clear. I not only came to egg it on, but to egg it on *now*, Mr. Lockwood. Sally's been—marking time, as she calls it, but why should she, after all? It only puts things off. If she breaks up her marriage now, it's something that had to come. And if it helps, that you've appeared on the scene then, then that could be a way out. The thing would be done and—at last would be over. Now, does that help, Mr. Lockwood?"

He didn't answer at once, but sat looking at her, and then at last said quite slowly: "*So what you're afraid of, what you're terrified of, wouldn't happen, would it?*"

"I—don't know what you mean."

"Yes, you do."

"I don't! I swear I don't! I——"

"Won't admit it, and I don't expect you to. You've made things clear just the same, and I get it at last, why you came. And all I can say is, I like you better and better."

38]

"And—I like you, Mr. Lockwood."

"What's your name, Mrs. Simone? Your first name."

"Grace."

"Mine's Clay."

"Yes, I know, and——"

"Grace, when Sally left last night, we didn't say good-by, and she may not know that that's what it was. Just the same, I won't see her again. But to let you get things straight, I didn't bring her here just for a few evenings' fun. The very first night, and last night too once again, I put it on the line—asked her to do what you want: make the break now, leave that guy, go to Reno and have it done. I even begged her to stay here with me. Her answer was I was nutty—that to do what I wanted she'd have to give up that dough, what she thinks she'll get of the fortune that Mr. El will leave, what she'll get and what her boy will get. But that wasn't all, Grace. It showed through, like the blue on a corpse's finger-nails, what she's hoping for. What she means to do, perhaps. *If* she gets help—of the kind she thinks I can give. I won't! Get that straight, Grace. I won't be her patsy."

"I haven't the faintest notion——"

"What I'm talking about. That's O.K."

"But if you took her *now*—?"

"I told you: I tried it. We're past that."

"But, Clay, you can't give up *that* easy!"

"Why can't I?"

"You're in love with her, that's why."

"What makes you think I am?"

"Clay, a woman knows. You give yourself away with every word you utter. When you draw your breath in you tremble. Did you know that?"

"So, I *could* be in love with her maybe."

"The one who could be *is*."

6

They talked a bit longer, repeating what had been said, but in a more matter-of-fact way, he helping her regain her aplomb, the crisp elegance she had had when she came, and then he took her down, as he thought, to her car. But on finding that she had come on foot, that she had walked from Rosemary Park, where she lived, he insisted on taking her home. So she hooked a hand on his arm and they strolled through the balmy spring night and, in snatches, talked. It was mostly about flowers, and she stopped occasionally to point out the splashes of color the azaleas made on the lawns or to stare at the leaves overhead, now half open, "so feathery, so delicate, so unreal—so like the *Midsummer Night's Dream* overture, those butterflies in the strings." She went on: "That play is *not* about summer—it's about spring, when everything's moist and fresh instead of all dried up, when the flowers are still singing and the locusts haven't started. But, of course, Midspring Night's Dream is not a title—even Shakespeare, no doubt, had to think of *that*." He agreed, glad he knew his Mendelssohn, and drew her attention to the splotches of white the dogwood blossoms made, "as though calcimined on." She said: "Yes, the original Chinese white." His hand was on hers as they reached her apartment house, another place like his own, if smaller. She stood peering in at the door, then whispered: "It *is* a beautiful night, and not the end of the story. I won't have it that way! You're *not* through with Sally—we have more talking to do! Would you like to come up for a while?"

"I'd love it."

She took him inside the automatic elevator, then brought him into her apartment, excusing herself after turning on the lights. He wandered about, eying the modernist furniture, the oyster-shell rug, the crimson drapes, the French things on the walls, prints, posters, sketches, and paintings. He scanned the signatures closely, but didn't see one that he knew. She came back with a highball tray, looking slenderer without her hat, gloves, and stole, and younger with her hair fluffed out on her neck. He spoke for Scotch on the rocks, and she filled a glass with ice, then let the whisky cover it. Making a light one for herself, she took a seat on the rectangular sofa, motioned him beside her. They sipped, recalling the dogwood again; then, recalling the overture, he hummed the violin part. She led him back once more to the "proposal" he'd made to Sally, and he told it in more detail, especially her answer to it, with due emphasis on the Wild Man from Borneo and nuttiness. He admitted he had been "rocked," and solemnly proclaimed how simple it all would have been if "she'd just done nothing at all—stayed there, tucked away with me, and let me handle the rest."

"If '*she*' had?"

"Well, who are we talking about?"

"Do you realize you almost never say her name?"

"O.K., I was hard hit."

"And still are?"

"Grace, I've told you I'm through."

She thought some moments, then said: "Clay, I'd like to work on you, try to sell you on Sally, that you make another attempt, to get her to do what you want—what we both want. So why don't I paint your portrait? After all, you are a thing of beauty, and you could come here at night, pose in my atelier, the little sun porch that I have, and while I work I'll talk. You'll be my captive audience—and who knows? I might make a sale."

"You could—one that you don't expect."

". . . What do you mean, Clay?"

"You're a thing of beauty too, don't forget."

"Clay, *she* has dibs on you."

"Dibs is dibs, of course. But—!"

"Stop talking like that, Clay."

"Where is this atelier, Grace?"

So they began doing his portrait while he half reclined on the window seat in the sun porch off her living room, and she worked with pencils first, doing endless sketches of him, "to get what's in your face—your eyes can be so fishy, except at certain times, and those times are what I want"; then she began working in color, with shiny tubes on a table and brushes laid beside them. At that stage she pushed out an easel, an upright post to which she clamped her board, already framed in raw oak, "so I can see what I'm doing." She had him wear a blue shirt, "to go with your eyes and bring them up," and a garnet jacket she had him buy, with brass buttons "to go with your hair." As she worked she talked, often about the child: "Don't forget, Elly's my grandson, Clay—something I can't get used to, but it's true just the same. And if I tell the truth, he concerns me most of all, and he's what it's really about, this campaign I'm pushing with you. Because he could really be blighted in case of some *mess*—or whatever it might be—that Sally got herself into."

But mostly she talked about Sally, her birth, her childhood, her venture into magic, her marriage, and what had come of it. She was helped by little promptings, queries of various kinds, from him, and before very long had told perhaps more than she meant to. So at the end of two or three

[43

weeks, with the portrait nearly done, he got up one night, for a stretch, from the window seat where she posed him and suddenly started to talk. "So," he said briskly, "as I get it, this sweet innocent child, barely turned seventeen, got herself sawed in half, but took no interest at all till she found out who he was, this guy in the sorcerer clothes—the son of the Gorsuch millions. Then she went into action, took a job in the act, married him, and at once gave him a son, who was also, we note, an heir. Then she started in making his life a hell on earth in the hope of getting a settlement. But what she got was a summons, an order from the court, sued out by her father-in-law, to show cause why she shouldn't be declared an unfit mother to her child. She won, by a hair, but then cooked up a real plan, which has you scared to death."

"I still don't know what you mean."
"That we understand. But your campaign hasn't worked, so why don't we get on—talk about you and me?"
"My campaign has worked, Clay."
"No—you talked just a little too much."
"You're in love with her, Clay."
"No, no more. Sorry."
"I can prove it—or think I can."
"Interesting if true . . . How?"
"By watching your face when I tell you . . ."
"Tell me? What, for instance?"
She came over, took him by the forelock, and peered into his eyes as she said: "She's going to be free this weekend." Then she laughed at his sudden intake of breath, which came with his startled blink, and went on: "Mr. El is taking Elly for the Memorial Day weekend—she'll have evenings for you and means to call you up. I know, as she asked me, when I dropped in for lunch at Portico, if I still had the number she'd given me, or need she give it to me again? I assured her I'd kept it. Now, have I proved it or not?"

"All you've proved is she's calling me up."

But his voice sounded thick, and she laughed once more as she dropped a cloth on the picture. "Why kid yourself?" she asked. "If you could see your face, you'd accept what it means."

"I tell you, I'm through."

"And *I* tell *you*, you're not."

The call came, at his office, she opening with the charge: "You louse, you've been ducking me—not answering your phone even once." He protested he hadn't been home; "we have all kinds of grief here at the goddam shop, refrigeration went on the fritz. I've been here every night." He was oddly breathless about it, but she didn't argue much, and quickly they arranged it, the dinner Friday night, she to arrive around seven, he to "do it big, with flowers and everything." So, for the next day or so he lived on expectation, ordering bunches of roses and bringing home extra-fine steak, caviar, mushrooms, and champagne. But on Friday something happened that stood his world on its head. He was just back at his desk, from his afternoon tour of inspection, when Miss Helm appeared at his side, leaned close, and whispered: "There's a Mr. Alexis to see you, with a girl. . . . Mr. Lockwood, it's the Great Alexis, I'm sure—you know, that guy at the Lilac Flamingo, the magician? And the girl, I think, is the one that works in his act. . . . Is something *wrong*, Mr. Lockwood?"

"Did he say what he wants, Miss Helm?"

"Well, I didn't ask him. Shall I?"

"No. And nothing's wrong. Send him in."

Mr. Alexis came in importantly, a tall, slender young man in smart summer suit, with a little eyebrow mustache and sharp, squinting expression. With him came a girl, a small, plump creature with light hair and twinkling eyes, whose outfit was certainly startling, consisting as it did of pink crepe dress with no sleeves, red socklets on bare legs, white kid shoes with high heels, and red band around her head. She smiled at Clay while her companion held out his hand, announcing with bland assurance: "Alexis, Mr. Lockwood—professionally known as the Great Alexis. You may have heard of me."

"Why—yes, I have," said Clay, gulping and after a moment taking the hand, then letting go after one pump.

"This is Miss Conlon—she works with me."

"Professionally known as Buster," said the girl, "and you *must* have heard of me."

"I have indeed," Clay assured her, taking the soft little paw she gave him. "I'm very glad to know you."

"Likewise," she said. "Very, very, very."

But as she looked Clay up and down with obvious interest, Mr. Alexis chided her: "You don't have to jump in his lap." He tried to sound facetious, but something ugly, perhaps of jealousy, showed through.

"Well, he hasn't asked me yet," she replied archly.

"Sit down, sit down, please!" Clay interjected, pushing up chairs, then resuming his own seat, in the chair back of the desk. Leaning back, he coached himself to say: "I'm sorry, you'll have to talk with my lawyer—I don't handle such things myself." He assumed this was about Sally, though what Buster had to do with it he had no idea at all. So he was confused when Mr. Alexis, his aplomb somewhat regained, said: "Mr. Lockwood, Mike Dominick sent me to you, on a matter that's come up that he said you could help me on, and might be willing, if I——"

"*Mike Dominick?*" Clay exclaimed.

"He runs the Lilac Flamingo, that Baltimore club where I work." And then, at Clay's astonished stare: "Well, look, if I'm in the wrong place, just run me out, Mr. Lockwood. Mike told me you were a friend."

"Well, yes. I sell him meat. But—"

"Something's wrong, I can see. So—"

"No, please!"

"You don't have to jump in his lap," said Buster to Mr. Alexis. "Give him time, let him readjust. How do you know? Maybe Mike has other names too—and not at all professional. They could be aliases, even. And——"

"I'm sorry," Clay apologized. "I'm not quite caught up, that's all. Let's start over. I know Mike, of course—I've known him for years, and he's right. He is a friend. How is the old *mafioso?*"

"About the same," said Mr. Alexis.

"Which is not saying much," Buster murmured.

"Practically nothing at all," Clay agreed. "He's O.K., just the same. What's this matter of yours, Mr. Alexis? The one you say has come up."

"It has to do with my act."

"And my neck," Buster explained.

"I see, I see," said Clay, though he didn't.

"Next week," Mr. Alexis continued, "we go on summer schedule, with half the place closed for redecoration all through July and then the other half through August—and of course for some alteration, which is where I come in. I have to have stuff put in for an act I hope to pull off, beginning in the fall. But I have to speak up now, so contracts can be let. Because, Mr. Lockwood, take magic—what's wrong with it, now?"

"Well—is anything?"

"No! And that, my friend, is what's wrong!"

"You have to work on it," Buster told Clay. "It doesn't get any better, but at least you can understand it."

"If you'd keep your mouth shut!" snapped Mr. Alexis.

"Your wish is my command," she told him, winking at Clay and zipping her mouth with her thumb.

Mr. Alexis now grew dramatic, asking Clay: "So what makes a variety act? The perfection of it? No! The things

[47

that *do* go wrong! Like on the wire, when the guy misses his somersault and has to take it over—that's what they eat up, isn't it? And with dogs, the one the people love is the little white pooch who won't go over the man, but runs between his legs! Even with cats, the tiger they go for is the one that balks at his jump and has to be coaxed with the whip. But with magic, what? Nothing ever goes wrong, and I say that's what's wrong. So, I've been working on it. All last season, in our levitation, Miss Conlon went up in the air. She floated, she rose, she came down—and that was all." And then in a whisper, leaning close: "I want this girl to get lost! So when I make my little speech, pick up the steel hoop, and turn to pass it over her, she's not there. She's disappeared. I ask for quiet, for absolute quiet—I request that nobody move, and begin calling to her. And then a woman screams. And then I see where she is—they all see where she is—floating up under the ceiling——"

"In my weightless condition," said Buster.

"But to do it," said Mr. Alexis, ignoring her, "I must have a movable cradle I can suspend her from, which must have something to run on and——"

"You want to look at our overhead stuff?"

"That's it! If I may, Mr. Lockwood!"

"Nothing to it—we'll look at it right now!"

Beads of sweat, of infinite relief, standing out on his brow, he took three coats from their hangers, gave one to Mr. Alexis, one to Buster, and slipped one on himself. Her zipper, as he pulled it up from the floor, ran over quite shapely contours, evoking her baby stare, which Mr. Alexis saw. However, nothing was said, and they trooped down to the storage room, where the rails, trolleys, and hooks excited Mr. Alexis greatly. He asked all sorts of questions about them, getting a card from his pocket and making note of the company that put such fixtures in. He inquired about strength, being assured by Clay "it's tested for tons, not pounds—has to be, as quarters of beef can get bunched, rolling along, so the strain on the rail is quite heavy. One quarter weighs two hundred pounds—more than Miss Conlon, I imagine." But when Mr. Alexis rolled one of the quarters an experimental foot or two, it made a dismaying rumble. Clay used the weighmaster's phone, told Miss Helm to come down "and bring some rubber bands—whole box, if it's there, of the biggest ones we have." When she got there with them, he took a hook off the rail, wrapped its roller in rubber, put it back again, and tried it. It rumbled scarcely at all. "Now we're coming!" said Mr. Alexis. "It's going to work, I can see that."

"I want to try it," said Buster.

"What for?" asked Mr. Alexis.

"Well, what do you think? After all, *I'm* going to be up there. Not somebody else, Alec—*me*. And I want to feel how it is."

She raised her arms, as though to be lifted up, but Mr. Alexis just stood there, not stepping forward to help. Prettily, she looked at Clay.

He lifted her.

She caught the rail, nodded.

She swung a little and jerked up and down.

"O.K.," she said, and Clay stepped forward to lift her down. To his astonishment, Mr. Alexis put out his arm, barring his way. "Not so fast," he told Clay. And then, to Buster: "You want down, let go. You'll come down."

"Well, thanks a lot," said Buster, her white kid shoes dangling. But when Clay moved to help her, Mr. Alexis stepped between. "*Hey!*" he growled, "*she's my girl!*"

"She's my guest," said Clay, "in my place. I just don't care to be sued if she falls and breaks a leg."

Shouldering Mr. Alexis aside, he took hold of Buster again and lowered her to the floor. There was a gritty moment, and

[49

then, to get things going again, as they had been before, he said: "There's just one thing: you should make sure, and check on it every few days, that it's absolutely level, whatever you have put in. I would use a spirit level and check on it myself, as that's going to be important, for control of your stuff up there, and also so it's *safe*." He told of a place in Mexico "where they put in all modern equipment, the best that York, Pennsylvania, puts out, and forgot one thing, alas: the way the foundations settle there on that filled land that Mexico City is built on. So this place settled too, so the cold room rails canted one hot weekend. Ten tons of meat rolled down on the end of a rail, so a bolt snapped from the weight and dumped it down on the pipes, jamming a valve. Brother, when they opened up Monday morning, was that a job for the buzzards. Spoiled meat can smell, in the heat of Mexico City, when reefer pipes go dead—and costs, if you know what I mean."

Ten minutes later, on the parking lot, his manner again suave though his face was still a bit grim, Mr. Alexis said good-by. "Thanks, Mr. Lockwood," he declaimed in his best platform voice, "you've been most helpful indeed—shown me just what I wanted. You're invited to my opening, as my guest, my personal guest."

"I—hope I can make it," said Clay.

"Likewise," said Buster. "Very."

"That does it—she's leaving him and leaving him now! God, what a heel, what a pompous, vain, and stupidly jealous heel! And what a dangerous heel! If you hadn't been there, he'd have popped that girl in the jaw! If you hadn't been bigger, he'd have popped YOU in the jaw! What a revelation of the life poor Sally has led!"

7

Poor Sally, when she got there after phoning she would be late, didn't quite look like herself. She was still in her Portico uniform, with little straw hat to match, but her crisp Portico style was not on view at all. The hat was askew, the dress mussed, the face slack. She was tacky, disheveled, and loose, and her mouth, wet with desire, plainly betrayed the reason. When he opened, she clamped her arms on his neck, started a long hot kiss, and lifted her heels from the floor, as though to be carried in the direction of love. He carried her, but into the living room, which was decked, to be sure, with several vases of roses and fragrant with toast, caviar, and crumbled egg—but it wasn't their regular dovecote. "Here!" he said, putting her down and waving at the comestibles. "You must be starved." She blinked, then told him: "Well, maybe I am—but not for this stuff, just yet. What's the matter? Don't you like me?" He said he liked her fine, "but we have some talking to do." She stared, then snarled: "What is this? I come for a little romance and you give me goddam fish eggs—and a song and dance about talking we have to do. What is this, anyway? *What* talking?"

"Your husband was in today."

"Alec?"

"Yes, Alec. He came to the shop."

She sank to a sofa, stunned. "And you spilled it?" she

whispered, licking her lips. "You told everything? After all I've said, you told him about me?"

"So happens I didn't."

Somewhat reassured, but not much, she braced to hear him out. In considerable detail, with special stress on the scene in the cold room, when he lifted Buster down, he told of the day's visitation and when he had finished said: *So!*"

"Well? So what?"

"Sally, can't you see?"

"Why, I can see how he shook you up, coming in that way, but once you knew what it was, why should it be such a bomb? So he needs overhead rails and Mike sends him to you? Why shouldn't he? After all, you do sell him meat, and after all you do have overhead rails. Maybe I'm dumb, but I don't get the dramatics."

"Then maybe you *are* dumb."

"So—to the dumb you have to explain."

"Don't you see? I took his hand."

"Well, did it have the pox on it, Clay?"

"I can't shake his hand and sleep up with his wife."

"You *are* sleeping up with his wife! Or *were*."

"I can't do it behind his back."

"You *did* do it behind his back—didn't you?"

"Listen, it started that way—things got out of hand. But from the beginning I wanted it out in the open. I begged you to go to Reno and never go back to him. You wouldn't, and things coasted along. O.K., but now they can't coast any more. Listen, it's like that O. Henry story where the guy couldn't drink with the man he blackmailed. I can't take a man's wife and then shake his hand. Listen: it's not taking the wife—I don't mind that at all. If he can't keep her, she's fair game for me—life is like that and I'm not even slightly ashamed. But shaking his hand, all at the same time—that's different. I won't do it, and now that it's happened, a whole new chapter has started."

"What O. Henry story?"

"Does it matter? I forget the title of it."

"It still makes no sense to me but— Let's get on, Clay. What new chapter? If you know."

"First, we go to him."

"And then?"

"Reno."

"At my expense?"

"Sally! I pay for it, of course. We——"

"Including the millions it costs me?"

"Oh, so that's it! It's been said now, at last!"

"It's *been* said from the beginning, Clay—the trouble is you don't listen. You pretend *nothing's* been said when it has been. Those millions, dear heart, are important. And so you get it straight, I'm not giving them up. Now, what else?"

"In the first place, you're not in line for the millions."

"So happens I think I am."

"In the second place, they're not all."

"You mean there's you and your lily-white hand?"

"Sally, I mean there's you, and your more or less lily-white life." And as she looked at him, startled, he went on: "I didn't like this guy, and from the start I felt something peculiar. The whole thing, his idea for the trick, his coming, his testing of the rail, had something phony about it. And quite a while after he left I hit on the explanation—to my own satisfaction, at least. You used to work for him, didn't you? In the act, before you had your baby? O.K., then—suppose Buster gets sick? Suppose she gets the flu? And he puts the bite on you to go on in her place? Sally, with you hanging up there by wires from a cradle on rails, your life will be hanging there too, and *I would not give a nickel for it!* That's what we have to think about, and believe me, once you come crashing down, there'll be no millions for you. Did you hear what I said? There won't be anything—but a bang-up funeral, with lilies. And I happen to love you, that's all."

[53

He had no recollection of having this idea at all before he started to talk, and in fact heard himself get it off with utter astonishment, mixed with some admiration. It was a pure, inspired ad-lib, but it got him nowhere at all. She listened with ill-concealed boredom and, when he was finished, said: "Well, thanks for worrying about me—though there was no reason, really. You were right, of course, about one thing: there was something phony about it. He's dreaming about this stunt, which he thinks will be quite a sensation. But to pull it every night, with her 'way up in the air, would get him in dutch with the cops—she's a human being, believe it or not, and they would worry about her—maybe haul him to court. So to take care of that he'll fake it—use a wire frame and plastic head, so she seems to be up there and isn't. But to tell you how it's done, as he figures, would be telling the whole wide world—and if that sounds silly to you, you don't know magicians. They think the world is lying awake to know how their tricks are done—they guard their secrets like gold. So to cover up, to make it all look kind of real, he brings *her* to see you too—as though she's the one to be reassured. But when she decided to chin herself on the rail, that was coming too thick. Now that was an idea, wasn't it? All she wanted was a feel—from you. And the way you tell it she got it—and I don't blame him for how he felt. He's a crumb, he's ruined my life—but for once I'm on his side."

"I'll never be on his side."

"All right—what else?"

He tramped around, very agitated, then turned to her and blurted: "We talk—we bat it around—we don't get anywhere. So I'm taking this bull by the horns. You're not going back."

"You mean, to him?"

"To him, to that house, or anywhere, but here. So, our new life begins—has begun—as of now. So why don't we celebrate?"

He went out in the kitchen, got a quart of champagne from the icebox, with glasses he had put there to chill. Coming back, he twisted the wire off the bottle, worked the cork with skillful fingers, got it out with a festive *pop*. He poured a sip in one glass, tasted, then filled both glasses and raised one with a flourish. "Happy days!" he declaimed. "To you, to Elly, to me. Happy years, happy—everything."

She made no move toward her glass. "Just goes to show," she observed after a moment, "how mistaken you can be. How mistaken *I* can be."

"Yeah? What mistakes have you made?"

"Oh, you know. Like with the rock I thought I had. Well? You looked like a rock, kind of. And acted like one—I thought. But the rock turned out to be more of a mock orange. Ever see one, Clay? Kind of pretty on the outside, like a big green grapefruit. Open it up it's not so good. Instead of juice it has milk, that's slimy and sticks to your fingers and stinks—so you want to throw up. Like what runs in your veins, come to think of it. What a rock. What a hero. What a joy. What a comfort—to a girl in trouble that needs someone to lean on."

"O.K., lean. I'm *here*—not there."

"*Damn it, shut up!*"

Though his finger trembled, betraying how much he was shaken, he pointed it at her glass, saying: "I toasted you 'Happy days.' What are you toasting me?"

She raised her glass, and he reached for his to clink. But then suddenly he was blinded, by wet stinging stuff in his eye, and realized she had thrown the wine at him. Wiping off with a napkin, he heard glass breaking, and when he could see, she was lunging at him with a stem, a glittering, splintered thing that she held in her fist, like a practiced barroom fighter. He jumped up and backed away. She jumped up and charged. Her next lunge grazed his cheek and he clipped her on the chin, toppling her over backward.

When he touched his tingling cheek his finger came away red, and he went back to the bathroom, stopping the blood with a styptic pencil. When he got back to the living room he gave a gasp of horror, for pictures, cups, and mementos were all on the floor, the caviar and egg were stamped into the rug, the champagne was upside down, gurgling into the sofa, and she was on his Orozco, the finest painting he had, which had hung over the fireplace, kicking the frame apart and grinding her heels in the canvas. He grabbed her and she cursed him, he flinching at the words, so different were they in her shrill feminine accents from their sound as said by men, and so horrible. Dragging her to the door, he pushed her out. Then, aiming with care, he drove a kick at her bottom, with all his strength, that sprawled her on her face in front of the elevator.

Coming back, he closed the door, panting from exertion and gagging from revulsion. He saw her bag on the telephone table. Grabbing it up, he opened the door again and threw it at her, where she still lay on the floor. Then, banging the door shut, he dived for the bathroom, where white foamy stuff came retching up from his stomach.

"You've had it—this is the end. You're not seeing this dame again for the rest of your life or of hers. You've seen her for what she is, and if you go on asking for more, you should have yourself committed. Did you hear what I said? You're through!"

8

Taking an armful of towels, he stuffed them into the sofa to sop up the wine. Then he gathered up paintings and bric-a-brac, including the Orozco, and piled them on the piano. Then he got yards of paper towels and went to work on the rug to clean up the mess. He heard, almost without emotion, a bedlam of screams outside, with kicks and thumps on his door, and did nothing about it at all. He had just finished, using dustpan and whiskbroom, brushing up the last of the egg, when his inside phone rang. People had made complaints, Doris coldly informed him, "from all over the building, about some woman up there, whooping and hollering and banging on your door." Dully he admitted, "She's out there in the hall, I guess." When Doris asked him what she should do, he answered foolishly that it was "your hall, not mine—do whatever you want." On her informing him, "In a case like this I have to call the police," he told her: "Why, sure, I guess you do." She talked a few moments more, making it clear to him the police were going to be called.

He hung up, put the chain lock on the door. Then, opening as far as the chain would permit, he called through the crack: "Cops are being called—they're on their way."

"*Ah, you would, wouldn't you?*"

He closed the door again, remembered the ham in the

oven, went in and turned it off. He waited for more kicks on his door, but none came, or any more screams, for that matter. Then his buzzer sounded, and a man's voice said: "Police." He opened for the officers, who said they had had a complaint, so pulling himself together, he tried to answer them sensibly. "Yes," he said, "there was a girl out there, putting on kind of a roughhouse, but she seems to have gone—I haven't heard her the last few minutes. She uses the freight elevator and may have gone out the back way." The officers went, after taking in the living room. His stomach contracted again, but when he got to the bathroom with it, he discovered the trouble was sobbing, not retching. He decided to go to bed, but having had his say to the mirror, he avoided it while undressing, and when he had on his pajamas, crawled into bed. After a long time he persuaded himself he could sleep. He was just dozing off, or thought he was, when his inside phone rang again. This time when he answered he was quite peevish to Doris, asking: "Yeah, what is it now?" She said she was sorry to bother him, but "a lady is here to see you—a Mrs. Simone, the same one as was here before. But if you want me to say you've retired—?" He told her no, to "send her up," then hurriedly got into his bathrobe and put on the living-room lights. Grace, when he opened, was in a dark summer suit, and stood in the hall for some moments, not responding to his pleasant "Come in."

"I'm not sure I'm going to," she said coldly. "I've come about Sally. She's been with me—she just left. And I think it's *rotten* what you did to her!"

"I regret I have only one boot to plant in her tail for my country. If this be treason, make the most of it!"

"She's horribly bruised, do you hear?"

"Maybe so, but the cops have been here once, and unless *you* want a ride in the wagon, you'd better come inside."

She came in then and at last saw the living room. She winced as though hit with a whip, wailing: "Oh! Oh! Oh!"

And then: "I—didn't know about this. She—didn't tell me about it! She didn't say one word!"

"Just told you what *I* did, hey?"

"Not by name. Just——"

"Called me a louse and went on from there?"

" 'Son of a bitch' is what she called you."

"Now, that sounds just like her."

By then she had reached the piano and begun examining the things piled on it. Seeing the Orozco, she started to cry, picking it up, touching fingers to it, turning it over, peering at the reverse side. Then, passionately: "It can be repaired—and I'll pay for it, Clay! There's a Mr. Gumpertz on Chase Street who'll make it as good as new! He does marvelous restorations! He——"

"I know Jake, of course. I'll call him—and pay my bills, if you don't mind. This one's going to be big."

"She . . . didn't mean any *harm!*"

"Of course not! Just her way of having fun!"

"Clay, please!"

"Grace, what did you come about?"

He had taken a seat on the sofa, the dry one with its back to the piano, and before answering, she came and sat beside him. Then she said: "I had to see you."

"To bawl me out."

"Yes."

"O.K. Go ahead."

"I can't—not after *that.*"

With a shudder, she motioned to the Orozco, and perhaps to ease things for her, he asked: "How's my picture coming along?"

"Rather well, I think—it's almost done now. I was having trouble with it—the eyes were slightly cold. They looked the way they *do* look when you have that stare on your face that you wear most of the time. I wanted that other look, that warm, interested look that you get when you want to be friendly. And it wouldn't come. But then something happened, I don't quite know what. The blade—on the face I'm using a knife—gave a flick, and there was one eye as I wanted it. Then the other one came—and I stopped. Except for some work on the hands, I'm done."

"I'm certainly curious to see it."

"What do I smell, Clay?"

"Ham. Want some?"

"I have to admit I didn't have much supper."

"I admit I didn't get any. Come on."

Huddled close at the dining-room table, she sipped white wine and wolfed down ham sandwiches. Presently her hand found his, and then suddenly gripped it. "Clay," she whispered, "you're going to ring her, aren't you? And say—something nice to her?"

"You mean, *now?*"

"She's home. And she's alone."

"Answer: no, Grace. I'm through with her."

"For me? I'm *so* frightened."

"Not for anyone. What are you frightened about?"

"I don't know. I keep telling myself about *nothing!* It doesn't help—I keep right on having these crazy jitters. . . . About her. About Alec. About Elly! About—*everything!*"

"The electric chair *is* frightening."

"No! Don't talk like that!"

"It's what you're afraid of, though—have been all along. It's why you came to me, in the hope I'd bust things up with this marriage she got herself into. Before things get out of hand. Do you know what started this thing? This brawl that we had tonight? It was because I was lousing her time schedule. She's marking time, she says, until the old man dies—and I wanted action tonight. I made my same old pitch, that she go to Reno, have it done, and marry me! But first I

60]

wanted that both of us go to him, that husband, and lay it on the line, how things stood, so he'd know—because something happened, Grace, that made it out of the question that things could go on as before, *in secret*." For the first time, then, he told of the afternoon's episode: "a damned unpleasant occurrence, and it opened my eyes to some things. The first was I don't blame her for all that's happened. That guy's an ugly customer and on top of that a fool. The second was—that fool, dunce, or jerk, I shook his hand. I made him my welcome guest, and that made it a new deal. Things can't go on as they were. But she, do you think she got the point? She just stared at me, as though I was some kind of a nut. I got tired of listening to her and laid the law down, but good. I told her how it would be, that she was staying with me and we would go on from there. We would start a new life, I said, and opened some wine to celebrate. She threw it in my face, broke the glass and cut my cheek, and wrecked my apartment for me. So if you think I'm calling her up, you just think again. I kicked her out, and she's lucky a boot in the tail is all she got from me. I should have—"

He broke off, speechless with the rage that had repossessed him, then asked: "Isn't that what you've wanted, Grace? Isn't that what you've asked me to do? Isn't it now? *Isn't it?*"

"Well, not quite in that tone of voice."

"My tone of voice was fine. Answer."

"Then, if you put it that way, I say yes."

"O.K. *Now!* Let's *us* go on from here."

"Meaning?"

"The same old thing I've meant with you from the start. Let's us begin 'going steady,' as the high-school kids call it."

"Clay, that's out of the question."

"You mean, you have to be loyal to her?"

"That, partly, of course."

"If she's out, what point does loyalty have?"

"*You're* not out, though."

She put out a hand, touched his bare neck, impulsively pulled him to her. "I own up," she said, "there's nothing I'd like better than to 'go steady' with you. Those weeks you sat for me—I made them last and last and last, I loved them so. And then the other night, when your eyes spoke to me, when I made them come alive, I knew the truth at last. But *my* love, Clay, isn't only desire. It can face sacrifice too—*must* face it if it's anything at all. And you've betrayed, with every word, how you feel about her—as she betrayed, when she came to me tonight, how she feels about *you!*"

"How she feels about losing her cat's-paw!"

"How she feels about—what?"

"You know what I mean, stop 'whatting' me. I'm sure she raged like a tiger, but it wasn't love, my sweet. She's not capable of it! She's——"

"*She is, she is, she is!*"

"I interrupted. I'm sorry. Go on."

"Whatever she's capable of, you're *in* this, Clay!"

"I *was* in it—not any more!"

"You're both in it!"

Both were panting as her chair inched closer and closer and her grip on his neck tightened. Then: "Clay," she whispered, "do you want to go on this way? The two of you fighting each other? With only one *possible* way for the whole thing to come out? It's not *whether* you make up! It's just a question of when! So why not do it tonight? Before you destroy each other, from pure, childish spite . . . Well, maybe not you. You're not vindictive, that I must say, my own wonderful Clay. But she is—she can't help it. That's how she was born, it's how she's going to die. If you won't destroy her, she'll surely destroy you, and that's the point it has, my loyalty to you! Clay, don't let it happen! Call her up, make a little gag, ask if it's turning blue, your heel mark on her bottom! So life can go on! So——"

"Behind his back, you mean?"

"Listen! That part can be straightened out!"

"With a blackjack it certainly can be!"

"Stop talking like that!"

"I'm talking like it is—what she's talking about!"

"I want to finish!"

"O.K. then, Grace—finish."

"Do you want to be ground to a pulp? Reduced to a nothing? Tortured so you won't even know your own name? So you can't think? We don't speak of selling meat—!"

"Oh, now I get it at last."

"Well, it's about time!"

He got up, put the ham away, washed their dishes, then went over to her and raised her face to his. "My sweet," he said, "my own beautiful Grace, *that's one thing you don't have to worry about!*"

"I rather imagine I do."

"I think we're going to be married."

"I can't even—hear what you said, Clay!"

"You did hear."

He had her wait while he went to the bedroom and dressed, then walked her home, through a night even more fragrant, beblossomed, and mad than the first night they had had, had been. "We're *going* to be married," he said, "whether you like it or not. But to prove I'm free to be married, that my soul isn't chained any more—I have to sell meat, don't I? Grace, it's going to *be* sold, all right. It's going to be sold right away, in a way it hasn't been sold, ever, in this town. Do you know what you've done? You've made me over, Grace—rededicated me."

"I wish I thought so."

"You'll see."

9

Twenty-four hours later he was staring at the sea, from the depths of a rocking chair, on the porch of a small hotel at Ocean City, Maryland—having driven there in flight from the frustration the holiday forced upon him. He had spent a sleepless night in a passion of high intention, with all sorts of fine schemes spinning around in his head, finding himself in the morning helpless to carry them out or even to do anything about his wrecked apartment. For fear his morale might ebb, and perhaps to preclude any call to Sally, he had packed his bag in a hurry and driven across the bridge that spans the bay, at length winding up at the sea. Here, to his relief, high purpose didn't recede, but gave way to dogged resolve, and so he had had a swim, in water just a bit cold, a dinner, and a nice, brooding sulk, and now was about to retire. However, he was joined by Mr. Reed, the hotel's proprietor, who took his meat and rated a sociable chat. In a quiet, easy way he made a standard gambit: "Nice place you got here—nice town, nice house, nice ocean"—but was just a bit startled at Mr. Reed's sour reply. "*Was* nice," he growled. "That's all we can say, Mr. Lockwood—we had a nice place once. Now all we got is a mess—a roughhouse, nothing else but."

"Oh? You mean this holiday thing?"

He was alluding to the problem at Ocean City, as at other

summer resorts, of teenage boys swarming in, so police have a job on their hands.

"That's the climax of it, yes."

But there seemed to be more, and Clay knew he must listen. "You know what it puts me in mind of?" Mr. Reed went on. "California, during a brush fire. Fellow was telling me, guy that lives out there, what it's like when they have one of them. It wasn't threatening him—it was up the slope a ways, where it couldn't possibly reach him. But his place was a short cut to it, so first comes it the bums, the extra help hired on by the state, to smack at it with their shovels, chop fire breaks, drag hose, squirt foam, and so on. Next comes it the bums' girl-friends, and turns out they have quite a few, very noisy and not very well behaved. Then comes it the ice-cream trucks, the beer vendors, and the hot-dog brigade, ringing bells and sticking pennants up in the grass. Then comes it the Iowa tourists, who never saw a brush fire, out to take pictures of it. Then comes it the TV bunch, out to take pictures of everything, including the Iowa tourists. So what can this guy do? He didn't start it—has nothing to do with it, really. But an Act of God is up there, a roaring, terrible fire. So maybe it does have beer cans around the edges, but if he squawks he's a heel—maybe an atheist, yet. So all he can do is get tromped—and that's how it is with us. *We* have an Act of God *too*—also with beer cans in front, an ocean that can roar as loud as a fire. And coming to see it are bums—not like in California, but bums just the same, in a way, *boys*. Not just a few, Mr. Lockwood, not just hundreds—*thousands*. And not only them but their girl-friends— what kind, I give you one guess. And not only them but the fly-by-nights, same as in California, with their ice cream, beer, and hot dogs. And tourists, *and* TV—giving the place a bad name. Three months from now, by Labor Day, when things come to a head, I don't blame our cops for cracking down or our judge for getting tough. Why should it happen to us? Can you tell me, Mr. Lockwood? We weren't doing nothing. We were just——"

"Hold on, Mr. Reed!" said Clay suddenly, taking his feet from the railing. "Hold everything! You've just given me an idea!"

"I sure hope so. What idea, Mr. Lockwood?"

"If you can't lick 'em, jine 'em!"

"*Jine* 'em? How?"

"*Sell* 'em! Ice cream. Beer. Dogs."

"Oh, I see what you mean. Unfortunately I'm in the hotel business—I sell a shore dinner, two-eighty-one with tax. And would those kids pay that? I give you one guess. On top of which, the way most of them dress, I wouldn't let 'em in. So——"

"In my business I sell what sells."

"You're leading to something, Mr. Lockwood. What?"

"I don't have the details yet—just a general idea, but as far as it goes, it's clear. As I see it now, the kids tromp you, the fly-by-nights take their money, and all you get is beer cans out on the edge of the ocean."

"That says it, that's exactly it!"

"Why don't you go for their money?"

"But how? I sell a shore dinner! I——"

"Wait! It's beginning to come!"

He took Mr. Reed by the arm and led him out to the boardwalk, then down some steps to the beach and out to the thundering surf. Then, after staring, he led back up the steps to the town, now having the first gay night of its new summer season, with neon signs lit up and orchestras sounding off. He kept on to the town's boat harbor, one much like Channel City's, the long inlet called Sinepuxent Bay, where various craft were tied up, prettily reflecting the lights. And as he walked he dreamed out loud: "I see it now, Mr. Reed—a corporation, locally owned—locally owned, I said, by you and a few of your friends—a right little, tight little syndicate that'll have a series of booths—awnings, pitched on the sand, with grills and freezers and counters where girls in candy-striped pants will wait on our teenage friends and throw the empty cans in a *hamper*. You sell 'em ice cream, hot dogs, and beer—while *I* sell you what you need, I and some of *my* friends." Mr. Reed, after raising the question of cash, "the capital we'll need," and being told, "Don't worry about it," began to like the idea, and presently Clay went on: "I see something else, Mr. Reed: this thing has a civic angle. It's going to help put an end to the trouble. Because, 'stead of fighting these kids you'll befriend them, and 'stead of fighting you they'll get with it! And on Labor Day what will it be? Just a sociable cookout, that's all."

The upshot of it was that when Clay drove back, early Tuesday morning, he took Mr. Reed along, and no sooner got to his office than he "set up" a lunch for that day, in the Chinquapin-Plaza Blue Room, for the two of them, with Mr. Lomack of Greenfield Dairies, Mr. Gordon of Gordon Bakeries, Mr. Katz of Restaurant Fixtures, and Mr. Heine of Chinquapin Brewery. By then, having it all clear in his mind, he was able to lay it out to these prospective purveyors in the briefest possible time, and almost at once to sell it, to Mr. Reed's hypnotized wonderment. In fact, he took it for granted they would come in, "as it's something that should have been started years and years ago." When he knew he had them, he went on: "On prices, stock, deliveries, all that inside baseball—forget it. They're nothing, and we're all equipped for what's to be done. So let's keep our eye on the main thing—it's a public-relations question, first, last, and all the time. We have to convince that town and everybody in it that this is their enterprise—it's not run by the fly-by-nights. The money stays in the town. It's new money, it comes to the town, it stays there! I would say, and I hope you concur, that before we set up one tent we should run a series of ads—in *The Pilot* of Channel City, which circulates down at the beach—laying the whole thing out, introducing ourselves, saying who we are, coming out in the open. *Then* we'll be ready to go!"

All concurred.

"The thing is going to take dough. I'm putting Grant's in for five thousand bucks—as a loan, Mr. Reed, repayable out of earnings, as, of course, I couldn't claim stock without misrepresenting to those people in Ocean City. It's their show, without strings. Are the rest of you guys in?"

After a startled moment, Mr. Lomack nodded and rapped with his knuckles. Mr. Gordon rapped. Mr. Katz rapped, and after thinking, Mr. Heine. "O.K.," said Clay briskly, "that gives them twenty-five grand, which ought to hold them—anyway, to start."

Back in the office, he learned from Miss Helm that "a Mrs. Simone called—wants you to call her, at Fisher's." Grace, when he got her, seemed upset, and asked: "Have you seen The Bosun today?"

"Oh? That columnist? On *The Pilot*?"

"You'd better have a look."

"I will. Hold on a minute, Grace."

He had noticed Miss Helm with the paper, and she let him have it at once, looking, he thought, rather sheepish. Finding The Bosun, he read:

What well-known magician, booked in a Baltimore club, is burning because his girlfriend has started to cheat, with a big sausage-and-porterhouse man, here in Channel City?

"Well?" he asked Grace. "So what?"

"You don't think it just happened, do you?"

"No, I think a bitch put it in, as part of a get-hunk campaign that you kindly warned me of. But don't let it worry you, Grace. I've been busy selling meat, tons and tons and tons of it—but this I can handle too, and when I do I'll ring you. How've you been?"

"I've been fine, thanks."

"I took a trip to the beach."

"I hope you enjoyed it."

Hanging up, he asked Miss Helm to call Mr. Iglehart, of *The Pilot* business office, and when Mr. Iglehart came on, he made himself most agreeable, recalling a previous meeting and bringing up the new project, with the space it was going to require for the ads in *The Pilot*. "And why I called," he went on, "we're going to need help, of course, your very valuable help, with layout and stuff like that, and I was wondering if I could come in? Take up some of your time and——"

"Come in? Mr. Lockwood, I'll come to you."

"Oh, would you? You mean, today?"

"Well—I can. I'll come right over now."

But Clay told Miss Helm: "When Mr. Iglehart comes, cool him off a while. It suits me that he waits." So in twenty minutes or so, a good-looking young man sat, staring through the glass, while Clay stared back fish-faced, making no move to ask him in. At last he came in, or at least put his head in the door, smiling: "Mr. Lockwood? Jim Iglehart, of *The Pilot*."

"Oh, yes," said Clay. "Come in."

"You called just now. About space."

"Did I? You must learn to take a rib."

"Rib? Mr. Lockwood, I don't get it—"

"It's O.K., don't give it a thought. There's always *The Baltimore Sun*, which has space for me too—and doesn't print lies about me, like this thing that I saw, after talking with you." He handed *The Pilot* over, and Mr. Iglehart read The Bosun. "Well!" he faltered. "I can see why you wouldn't like it, but—after all, Mr. Lockwood, it doesn't *name* anyone!"

"Oh, how considerate," said Clay.

"And it doesn't *have* to mean you!"

"Just what I told my girl—my secretary—just now. And yet they were both in, the magician and his girl. I never saw either one of them, before or since, but—they were here. And so, not only my girl but every girl in the place thinks I'm a wolf, a chaser, a——"

"Will you give me five minutes, sir?"

"Sure, I'll give you till hell freezes over!"

"Will you give me a *phone* to use?"

"Help yourself, help yourself!" Clay said it sourly, waved at the phone, and walked out, winking at Miss Helm and telling her: "See that he gets his call—and let me know when he's done talking. I'll be down at the weighmaster's desk."

He clumped down the stairs and stood watching the meat go out, over the weighmaster's scales. Soon the phone rang and Miss Helm told him: "He's finished, Mr. Lockwood—and wants to speak with you."

Going back, he found a demoralized young man wiping his brow and massaging his mouth. "Sir," he said, "if you think that's easy, getting a paper to take something back, you ought to try it once. . . . They're killing it in the five-thirty, and tomorrow they'll run the retraction."

"Tomorrow? Why not *today?*"

"Why—to catch the editions that *had* it."

"I want it retracted *now!*"

"Well—that'll suit *them* a lot better!"

Why Clay preferred one edition today, for people who missed the original item, to several editions tomorrow, reaching those who had seen it, he didn't say, and perhaps didn't quite know. But the question of immediacy, of a gloating call to Grace, before she left her office, may have bulked large in his mind. He stood by while Mr. Iglehart called *The Pilot* again, talked briefly, and announced: "It's all fixed up—be in the five-thirty"—and then promised: "O.K., we'll talk about space tomorrow." Then, until the 5:30 would come, he filled in the interim with calls to Mr. Gumpertz, the furniture people, and the rug dealers, to have his stuff taken out—and with one to Miss Homan, the day girl at the Marlborough, arranging to have them admitted next day when they came. Then he called the Chinquapin-Plaza to reserve a suite for the night, it occurring to him that since his bag was packed and already in the car, he needn't go home just yet and look at the wreckage once more.

At last, Miss Helm brought the 5:30, and sure enough, the item was out of The Bosun's column, and beside it was a box:

Correction

In earlier editions, The Bosun alleged "cheating" by an unidentified girl with an unidentified man. The Pilot *has been unable to substantiate this, and regrets its publication.*

It didn't really say much, wasn't quite what had been promised, and perhaps left the waters more roiled than they would have been had nothing been said. But he had hardly finished it when he had Miss Helm call Grace, and when she came on the line blurted: "Read your five-thirty, Grace—you'll get quite a surprise."

"I've just finished reading it, Clay."

"Proves something, doesn't it?"

"Yes, indeed—that you're hardly able to talk. Whatever she does or doesn't do, it seems to wind up the same way."

"To me it proves she did not get away with a thing. She might just as well not have tried lousing me up. And, I am selling meat, did you hear me?"

"Then, if you're satisfied, fine."

"What are you doing tonight?"

"Why—nothing, I guess."

72]

"Dinner?"

"At your place? I won't go out."

"Temporarily I'm at the Chinquapin-Plaza."

He explained about his arrangements, and she said: "Then, if it's to be in your suite, and I'm not on public view, I'd like it very much."

"You'll come on your way from work?"

"I'll go home and change first."

10

For the next month or more he sold meat in a sort of frenzy, extending his beach involvement to Rehoboth, Delaware, and two places in Virginia, and moving not only frankfurters by the truckload but small steaks too, with patties of ground meat, lamb cut up for shashlik, and ham, tongue, and dried meat, packaged and sliced for sandwiches. He landed a drugstore chain, and then put over a coup, with a frankfurter commitment from Snax, which had the ball-park concession, and ran into trouble one day when a number of people fell ill, and had to be hauled off to the hospital, from eating dogs supplied by a Grant's competitor. Almost nightly he exulted to Grace, either at the hotel, where he stayed two or three weeks, or the apartment, when it was put in order again. She kept up her propaganda, to reunite him with Sally, but he wouldn't have it, even at the news she was free again, with the child at his grandfather's, at his beachhouse, for the summer. "I'm laughing at you," he said. "What's it to me, Grace, whether she's free or not?" He continued proposing marriage, but though tempted, she continued holding back. "But why?" he wanted to know. "How long do I have to prove that she means nothing to me? How much meat do I have to sell?" But she insisted that "All you're proving is that you're still in love with her."

And then one day, when he was just back from lunch,

Miss Helm informed him: "Mrs. Granlund's on the line—wants to speak with you."

"Bunny!" he gushed, taking the phone. "Long time no see no hear no touch! Why in the world——"

"*Clay!*" cried a shrill, overbred, domineering voice. "I'm expecting Pat Grant tomorrow! At twelve-thirty! For lunch! Do you hear?" Before he could answer, it went on: "He must come without fail, tell him! I'm asking quite a few people, and as he's to be guest of honor, I'll not have any excuses—no last-minute changes of mind, no politely wired regrets, with flowers. He's to come without fail, *without fail*, WITHOUT FAIL!" And, apparently as an afterthought, she added: "And of course you're included, dear Clay—I expect you to bring him yourself."

"But, Bunny," he broke in at last, after several tries, "Pat's not here! He's in Mankato! And I don't quite see how——"

"He's here! He's here in Channel City!"

"Whatever you say—but he's not."

"And you will bring him, Clay? Without fail?"

"I'll do what I can, of course."

Hanging up, he groused to Miss Helm about "the society mind—it's as brittle as cut glass." But as she laughed and turned to go, Mr. Grant himself walked in, a blocky, good-looking man in his thirties, in gabardines and beret. Blowing Miss Helm a kiss, he held out his hand to Clay, chirping: "Dr. Lockwood, I presume?"

"O.K., Stanley, it's me," said Clay, giving the hand a not-too-friendly jerk. "But what's the big idea? Spreading it all around. So everybody knows except me?"

"Who's everybody?"

"Bunny Granlund, for one."

"I haven't seen Bunny Granlund."

"She knows. She's invited you—to lunch."

"Well, Clay? Hotel coffee shop's a Portico thing, isn't it? Maybe they have a grapevine. Maybe I was seen by someone she knows. Maybe she's like a condor and knows without knowing how. Or maybe——"

"I'm mollified, forget it. I *guess* I am."

"Well, look, I bring a big surprise, and how can I do that and let you know all at the same time?"

"Then—let's have the surprise."

"Hey! Not yet! Red-carpet me!"

"Red carpets, please," Clay told Miss Helm, who was still standing there, smiling. "Our best Corona-Coronas." And to Pat: "I keep 'em with the meat, to have that exact humidity."

"No better place for cigars."

When the coronas had been brought, and Mrs. Granlund had been called, by Pat, with a pleasant, gracious acceptance, Clay again pressed for the surprise, but Pat seemed strangely diffident, and they went out to have dinner. On the way to the club they stopped at the apartment, where Pat played Bach and admired Clay's pictures, now back from Mr. Gumpertz and in place again. At dinner, out on the balcony, he talked and talked and talked without coming to the point—about Clay's baseball-park triumph, over his bad-hot-dog competitor, about the crab cakes they were having, about Château Yquem with apple pie, "a combo so queer it's weird, but the strange part is, it's *good*." And as Clay began to fidget he suddenly burst out: "Hey! This is the worst night of my life! So let me enjoy it, will you?"

"What's so bad about it?"

"For once I'm owning up to the truth."

"That I'm fired? Is that it? That's the surprise?"

"What makes you think so, Clay?"

"We're in for upward of fifteen grand on these beach commitments of mine—but I endorsed those drafts myself. They stand as my personal chits. So—"

"What the hell are you talking about?"

"Backing those beach corporations."

"Well, why not? We should have done it before."

"Well, get to it. What is this, Pat?"

" . . . You're not fired—I am."

"You? You own the goddam outfit—don't you?"

"Well, yeah—but what's to own, Clay, without somebody runs it that knows what to do with meat—besides eat it?"

"So? Don't you?"

"Stop being funny, Clay."

"So O.K., you went to Harvard. But Svenson knows."

"Yes, but Sven's turning seventy this week."

"No. I didn't realize he was that far along."

"So he has to retire, and at long last, Clay, I'm relinquishing him the title—president. Moving on to board chairman, putting an end to this comedy I've been playing, of being a big meat packer, of pretending that's what I am, when all the time I'm just third-generation rich, that can play Bach on your Steinway, honor Bunny with my presence, so all her friends will know I knew her at Bar Harbor, before her shoes got run down and she had to marry Steve, and talk about Château Yquem. Or in other words, I'll quit being a fake. As of next week, Sven will be president, and as of the first of the year, he'll be our beloved emeritus."

"Pat, it's damned decent of you."

"Been decenter ten years ago."

"Yet I don't mind saying, it gives me some concern."

"In what way, gives you concern, Clay?"

"Who's to follow Sven?"

"Oh, *that*—yes, I see what you mean and I'm glad you brought it up. I've given it considerable thought, and as I see it, we need a commanding type, a guy with a loud voice, a fist like a Grant gold-medal ham, a thick neck, an aggressive way with the clients, and a mania for selling meat in eighteen different ways that never were thought of before, most of them vulgar, pushing, and rude. Or in other words, Clay, you."

" . . . *Me?*"

78]

"Now you know. That's the surprise."

"Revive me, please. I think I just fainted."

Pat talked on, about the rigors of being a fake and the shame of "living a lie," apparently seeing himself as a tragic figure, but sounding more like a playboy, somewhat loquacious from wine, crying into his glass. Clay hardly heard him. He stared out at the pink of the sunset, the blue of the bay, and the white of the dipping sails, until everything blended together into a polychromatic euphoria, indescribably romantic and almost unbearably beautiful. His mood persisted after they reached the apartment, where they went for a sociable nightcap, as Pat's did too, he playing Bach again, and then switching to Gershwin's *Rhapsody,* whose opening he called "a real pronouncement on life—it's *laugh-clown-laugh, blow-blow-thou-winter-wind,* and *bye-bye-blackbird* all rolled into one." Clay agreed, and Pat finished the *Rhapsody,* then went on to "I Got Rhythm" and "Lady Be Good." Then a call came, and when Clay answered, *The Pilot* city desk told him they had heard a rumor, "a tip from Mankato, Minnesota, that you're to be president of Grant's. Anything to it?" Pat talked, to confirm, and soon a reporter came, accompanied by a photographer, when Clay took the floor, suddenly very important. "There's a revolution in meat," he proclaimed, as though making a speech to Rotary, though pausing every so often so the reporter could catch up with his notes. "We've come a long way since Grant's was founded in the northwest Land o' Lakes, because that's where the ice was, just as it was at Chicago, that they cut in winter, stored till summer, and chilled the meat with. Now there's ice all over, but the revolution goes on—in storing, cutting, packing, and, most of all, distributing. And so far as Grant's is concerned, we don't follow that revolution—we lead it. We're in the forefront of it—have been, are still, and will be."

The photographer hustled out to develop his film, and then the reporter left. Pat brooded, finally remarking: "That proves it, Clay, what I was saying before. Because while you seized the opportunity and said what the moment called for, what was I doing? Looking at your pictures and grappling with the problem of who's to paint your portrait. All Grant's, Inc., presidents are done in oil for the board room, with fingers suitably stuck into their coat lapel: my grandfather, like Washington crossing the Rubicon; my father, like Lincoln at Valley Forge, and me, like Napoleon at Appomattox. I'll get to Sven next, but that still is going to leave you. However, God willing, I hope—"

"Suppose I had a candidate?"

"Well, now, that would be a help. Who is he?"

"So happens, it's a she."

"Ah! Ah! Ah!"

"For this job how much do you pay?"

"Four-figure money, I think."

"Consider your problem solved."

He could hardly wait, when Pat took a cab to the hotel, to call Grace. She seemed a bit sleepy, even a bit grumpy, but eagerly he poured out the news of his luck. "Maybe I shouldn't have waked you up," he admitted, "but I wanted to tell you myself, before you saw the papers—and this is the first chance I've had. Pat has just gone home."

"Well! I'm certainly glad."

"But, Grace, that isn't all there is to tell!"

Bubbling with excitement, he told about the picture, saying: "Of course, *we* know it's done, but they don't—Grant's, I mean. And, Grace, they'll pay! Four-figure money, he said, which is at least a thousand dollars. Is that worth waking up for? *Is* it?"

" . . . I imagine it better wait."

"Wait? For what?"

"Till you've straightened things out with Sally."

"Sally? What does *she* have to do with it?"

"Haven't you told her?"

"No, and I don't intend to!"

"Clay, you'd better."

"Are you starting *that* over again? *Why?*"

"For the same old reason: you're in love with her. And, for another reason, Clay: she's going to be at the party!"

" . . . You mean—*Bunny's?*"

"I picked out her dress this afternoon."

"I'm sorry I woke you, Grace."

"You stay away from that party, dumbbell. Did you hear what I said? Let Pat go there alone—send Bunny three dozen roses, five dozen, ten. Don't go, don't go, don't go!"

11

The Granlund house, known as "Calvert Hall," was a fine specimen of old Maryland architecture, as well as an object lesson in the difference between things as they are and things as they seem, if adroitly distorted. From Queen Caroline Street, seen at a distance, screened by shrubbery and dwarfed by stately trees, it seemed modest in size, even small. It was of brick painted white, and in five sections: a center hall, two wings a short distance off, and two "hyphens" connecting. Its lines were thus broken, in the form of a careless sprawl, or what appeared to be a sprawl. Close up, however, from the rose garden out front, the illusion of happenstance, of small informality, vanished, and reality appeared, in the form of a stately, full-fashioned mansion. Ordinarily Clay loved it, though just as ironical as anyone at the recency of the Granlund tenure, and he often stood admiring it, perhaps imagining himself as owning it or some place not too unlike it some time in the future. Today, however, as he pulled up on the oyster-shell drive, all he could see was Sally's coupe parked near the door. It was the only car out there, as Pat had reminded Clay that he was the guest of honor, and as such bound to come early, "as a grand entrance later just louses the hostess up." So no one else had come, and Clay was even more nervous than he had been at the office, during a hectic morning hour of shaking hands with everyone.

And sure enough, once a colored functionary had let them in, she met them in the hall, trim in a black silk print with red poinsettias, holding her hand out to Pat. "Mr. Grant," she said prettily, "welcome to Calvert Hall—I'm Mrs. Alexis, and I'll present you to the Granlunds." Then, turning to Clay: "Mr. Lockwood, so nice of you to come, so nice to see you again." She didn't shake hands with him, and he made no effort to. Holding up a finger to wait, she went to the great arch of the east hyphen and stood as though waiting for some signal. "Clay," whispered Pat, "I see good manners aplenty—it's all you do see nowadays. I don't see easy manners—but that girl *has 'em.*" Clay agreed, fighting off pride in her. Then she nodded to someone, came over, took Pat's arm, and led through the hyphen, a bower of green things in boxes, to the great drawing room beyond. There the Granlunds were drawn up in the middle of the floor: Mrs. Bunny Granlund, a large woman of forty, who proclaimed every whim, endearment, confidence, joke, and considered opinion at the top of her lungs, as though all within earshot were deaf; Mr. Steve Granlund, a tall, dour man, with the icy affability that seems to be the interchangeable mark of grand dukes, bishops, and headwaiters. He greeted Pat cordially and congratulated Clay on his promotion, which he had read about in *The Pilot.* Mrs. Granlund fell on Pat's neck, then put her arms around Clay, calling him "Dear boy" and "Our own Clay."

When she had placed Pat beside her, where the guests could be presented, Clay wandered off to a corner, relieved that nothing special seemed to be expected of him. There Sally followed, telling him: "Bunny asked me to take you in, as your partner, for lunch—and I said I would. Was that all right?"

"Why, yes," he said, sounding queer. "Sure."

"Well, you don't act very pleased."

"I'm surprised, that's all, that you'd want to take somebody in that had mock-orange juice in his veins."

"Mock-orange love is what I got—I'll say it was quite a letdown. But who am I to complain? If at first you don't succeed, try, try again."

"Now, what's that supposed to mean?"

"You'd like to know, I bet."

Her look had guile in it, and he tried to growl something, but nothing seemed to come. Then, lamely, he said: "So—I guess we're partners."

"O.K.—wait for me."

The guests, when they began arriving, were mainly men, bringing regrets from wives all over the earth, the sea, the mountains, and Europe. But a few women came too, heavily sunburned, in silk, cotton, and linen suits, all eager to help Mrs. Granlund prove her distinguished origin, before she invested it in restaurant millions. Service, at tables for four in the big dining room, was by a Washington caterer, with elegant Negro help, and not by the Portico staff, which for such an affair was a bit on the folksy side. But Sally had a table for two by the wall near the kitchen door, and from this post of vantage steered things with sharp efficiency. Under these conditions not much could be said, and Clay made no effort to say it, retiring into silence and resuming the sulk that had slipped without his meaning it to. But presently, during a lull, Sally asked in a casual way: "When is he going back? Your most likable Mr. Grant."

"He's taking the four-o'clock plane."

"You mean, today?"

"From Friendship. I'm riding him there myself."

"Then you *could* be free tonight?"

He looked up to find her staring at him in an arch, innocent way. "I could be," he answered gruffly. "I *am*. Why?"

"I could pay you a visit. I still have my key."

He was too shaken for some moments to trust himself to look at her. Then he did, and told her: "I'm sure you could, but you're not going to until quite a few things are explained."

"If you mean what I did to your place," she whispered, leaning close, "I'm not sorry for that—I'm glad. Listen, when I go to you, in the frame of mind I was in, and *you*——"

"There's also that piece in the paper!"

"What piece in the paper?"

He recited The Bosun's item, and she said: "So you think I tipped him off? All the trouble that that caused *me*? Do you know what it almost caused? Him breaking *off* with her—he began making passes at me. Well you *must* think I'm dumb!"

"O.K., we don't say any more."

"Oh, yes, we do—we say plenty, now that you've brought the subject up, of what I may have done, with good cause, Mr. Lockwood. Where were you? Why didn't you answer your phone?"

"Oh! So you called me!"

"No, Clay, I *rang* you."

The difference, it seemed, was profound. Calling, wanting to talk, was one thing, she explained in close detail. Ringing him, "making you answer your phone, and then hanging up on you, so you'd never get any sleep—that was something else." But, she finished, "you never answered your phone. Where were you? Playing around with Buster? Or what?"

"Bunny's looking at you."

She laughed gaily for Bunny's eye, then repeated, leaning close: "Where were you? You louse, I want to know!"

"At the Chinquapin-Plaza."

"So that was it!"

As he explained she indulged in retroactive rage, at the trick he had played her in not being home in person to suffer the vengeance she'd planned, he in a retroactive gloat at the neat way he had foiled her intention. But retroactivity is fleeting and of low voltage, so presently they laughed, and she said: "So all right, all right, all right. We'll say no more."

"Not so fast, not so fast!"

"Oh, for God's sake, Clay! What is it now?"

"You can come—I can't very well stop you. I might even be glad to see you. But it's mock-orange love for you unless you meet my condition."

"Condition? What condition?"

"Sally, the same old one."

"Oh? The Wild-Man-from-Borneo thing? Break up my marriage right away? Go to Reno and all that stuff?"

"That's it. You've got it."

"Well, I have to now, of course."

He was astonished, staring to make sure she was serious. She seemed to be, and he asked: "What do you mean, 'now'?"

"You're going away, I suppose?"

"That's right. And soon."

"Then you could walk out on me."

"Could? I have."

"Aw! Aw! Listen at him—walked out on me! My, I can hardly bear it! Well, you could come walking back, if I know you—and me. I imagine I just about know how to make you!"

"Get back to the subject. My going away—?"

"Compels me to make a choice."

"What choice, Sally? What are you talking about?"

"Well, there's you. And there's—!"

"The money?"

"*Yes!*"

For the first time she showed real emotion, her lips twitching, her eyes filling up. After some moments, getting herself under control, she went on: "Not that I like it, giving up twelve million bucks, but if it's that or giving you up—I guess I've made up my mind. I just don't think I'd like it, living my life without you. So, I've decided on *you*. I only hope you're worth it."

"Listen: I could be, at that!"

"You were always so modest, Clay!"

"I'm talking about the dough I could very well make before your life is lived. Sally, I'm on my way."

"Then, maybe I've done the right thing."

"I'll be home before five."

They sat studying each other, and then suddenly she said: "O.K., that's it, so let's cut out the jibbering and jabbering, and get down to brass tacks. I'm agreeable, and fact of the matter, I'd already made up my mind, before it all came out, what's in the paper today. *But,* I have to think of my child. He's with his grandfather, has been since Fourth of July, at the beachhouse on Brice's Point, and if I take off now and leave him there, he's just a hostage to hate, something to torture me with—in ways I couldn't think up but a spiteful old man can. So I have to get my baby. So you hold everything now until I find out from Bunny, before this thing breaks up, if she'll let me bring him to her and then take him with her tomorrow, when she leaves for Cape May, where her kids already are. Or in other words, if she'll do that for me, I'll go get Elly this evening and then later come to you—not forgetting, of course, I'm due at five o'clock, for a few minutes with you, if you still think you want to see me. Now, am I making sense or not?"

"Sounds A-O.K. with me."

"I'll see her and let you know."

They got separated, though, when the party spilled out on the lawn, where the photographers were "setting up," to have the advantage of sunlight. For some time Clay had to pose, with Bunny, Steve, and Pat, and then Pat grabbed his arm, dragging him up to say good-by. "We have to get out!"

he whispered. "Or these people are stuck—no one can go till the guest of honor does. That's me—*I'm him!* You keep forgetting my unusual eminence!" So, in a matter of seconds, Clay was pumping Bunny's thick hand and then Steve's thin one. He still hadn't settled things with Sally, but then, beyond bobbing heads, she gave him a little wigwag and held up five meaningful fingers. He drove happily, in a fuzzy haze, all the way to the hotel. There Pat had to pack and was so fumble-fingered about it that Clay had a horrible fear he would miss the plane and knock his date in the head. However, by calling a bellboy to help, they finally got the job done, and made the plane by a hair. Clay got home at a quarter to five, but as he opened the door caught a familiar fragrance. When he looked she was there, on the reconditioned sofa, a beckoning hand extended. Hungrily, ecstatically, he wrapped her in his arms.

Their few minutes stretched to an hour, and then she scurried off, "to pick up some things at home that my baby's going to need—and change my dress, while I'm at it." He ate uptown, at the Chinquapin-Plaza, mainly to kill time until she returned. He was back by early evening and decided he ought to call Grace. "So O.K.," he told her, "you win your bet—congratulations."

"What bet, Clay?"

"About me. About her. About—"

"Oh! You made it up?"

"Everything's settled, Grace. She's come to her senses at last. She's doing it my way—breaking her marriage up *now*, having it done in Reno, which of course has been your way all along."

"I'm so glad! It makes me so happy I want to cry. . . . And—so jealous I want to scream. Do you hear? I'd like to tear your eyes out!"

"That part is my one regret."

"Clay, you don't have any regret!"

"Well, listen, we've been pretty close."

"It's up to me to do my own weeping."

"Then, if you want it that way—?"

"It's not what I want. It's what has to be!"

He particularized a little, telling of Sally's meekness in acceding to his terms, her immediate plans for the child, and so on. Then he went on: "But I would say, Grace, we've come to a certain point, about family relationships. You and I will have to meet, and I thought the portrait could be the bridge. I mean, I could tell her what Pat said and ask if she knew anyone qualified to accept the commission. She'll have to nominate you—or at least, as we would think. And that'll do it. Do you agree?"

"Well—is a bridge really needed, Clay?"

"Well—I was just bubble-gumming."

"Can't we defer it, Clay?"

"O.K.—we let things take their course."

"Once again: I'm glad."

12

He played the Beethoven *Third* and the Tchaikovsky *Sixth*, and then, glancing at his watch, was startled to find it nearly eleven. She had said "somewhere around ten," which gave her ample time, as Brice's Point was a small place on the bay, an exclusive summer colony, a half hour's drive from town, so allowing for all delays, for argument, even for quarreling, four hours should have sufficed. He tramped around, a feeling growing on him that something had gone wrong. At last, looking up Elwood P. Gorsuch in the phone book and choosing the one at Ch's'p'ke Av of the three residences listed, he rang it. He had to hold on for a number of rings before a woman answered, seemingly much upset. She said, when he asked for Mrs. Alexis, "She's not here—nobody's here—there's nobody here to talk." By now greatly alarmed, he looked up the Alexis home and, for the first time, rang it. At once a man answered, and in panic he hung up. Then, in a helpless, demoralized state, he felt he had to call Grace. She listened, agreeing they had to do something, and told him to wait, not to make any more calls, "to keep your line clear," and she'd call him back.

In a few minutes she did, telling him: "At least I found out what it's about. Mr. El is dead—he died in Channel City Hospital, where they brought him after he choked on a nut. He always ate nuts and raisins after dinner, slapping great handfuls into his mouth, spite of everyone begging him not to—and tonight it happened, that's all. . . . *Or at least so Bunny Granlund says!*" In spite of herself, Grace wailed it, and then went on to explain: "I called the Alexis house, and the man who answered the call, probably the one you heard too, wasn't Alec. When he started pumping me, trying to find out who I was, I hung up, as he sounded to me like police. That's when I got the bright idea of giving Bunny a ring, and she told me what she knew. It seems that Mary MacReady, Mr. El's nurse, the woman who answered you, had taken a night off when Sally showed up, and Sally put Elly to bed. Then she went out in the kitchen to make some iced tea. While out there she heard something, and when she went in the living room, Mr. El was on the floor, not able to get his breath. She thumped him on the back and, when that didn't help, called the police to beg them to get her an ambulance. They did, and she rode in the ambulance, taking Elly along. But poor Mr. El was dead when they got to the hospital. Then Sally called Bunny, who took my little darling, God bless her—and that's all that she knows. But, Clay, is that all? What are police doing there with Sally at home? Or are they police? Or——"

"You'd like to find out, wouldn't you?"

"I'd give *anything* to."

"O.K., let's do it together."

He said that driving past the house "ought to tell us *something*," and she volunteered her car, as she kept it out on the street. He walked to Rosemary Park, and she met him downstairs in the lobby, in dark blue pima suit, somber and businesslike. She threaded the residential street, a route strange to him, but then suddenly popped on the Harlow Theater, now dark. She rolled down the familiar street, and as they approached the house Clay spotted white sedans in the drive. "There they are!" he whispered. "Those are police cars."

She kept eyes left as they drove, and suddenly murmured: "They're out there, talking—and that's Alec with them!"

"They must have reached him, then."

"*Clay, what's it about?*"

"Maybe nothing. On a thing of this kind, don't forget, they have to investigate—there's an autopsy and all kinds of stuff. Doesn't *have* to mean anything. Spite of the red tape, it could be mainly routine. And we can't help tonight. All we can do, Grace, is louse her."

"You mean we have to wait?"

"Till she gets in touch with *us*."

She dropped him at the Marlborough, so upset she didn't say good night, and he went to bed, though not to sleep. It was around nine the next morning, and he had just finished dressing, when Miss Homan rang him to say a lady was there to see him. Grace, when he let her in, was gay in red-checked gingham, and explained: "I didn't know what was coming and—wanted to look casual, as though nothing had happened. As though nothing possibly *could.*"

She had the paper with her and had thoughtfully bought two, so they both could read. Silently, side by side, they went through the main item, finding little in it that added to what they knew. The police, they learned, would "question Mrs. Alexis today," when the autopsy would be completed and its results known. "So," said Clay at length, "you got all worked up over nothing."

"I'm still all worked up."

"Over *what?*"

"Why are they questioning her?"

"Why not? She found him. They have to."

"Clay, I'm frightened to death."

"Have you talked to Sally yet?"

"For a minute, over the phone."

"And what did she say?"

"That 'it served him right'—for whapping the nuts in his mouth, I suppose she meant. 'Like a porpoise,' she called it. And *that* frightened me, too. Perhaps she didn't like him, perhaps nobody did, but her phone could be—what do they call it, Clay? 'Bugged,' I think is the word. And besides, he's dead."

"You can't exactly blame her."

"*I* can! She shouldn't talk like that!"

He continued offering her reassurance, perhaps a bit in excess of what he really felt, and then she broke in to cut him off. Opening the paper to an inside page, she pointed to a box beside the jump head and told him: "All right, you want to know why I'm worked up—*that's* why. I don't think you read it. You'd better."

The heading was "*Skeeter Tox Baffles Police,*" and the item told how officers answering the call had been perplexed by a smell in the air, which they took to be ether. It seemed that Sally confirmed this, explaining how she happened to have a bottle of ether with her. Her husband, she said, had had a rabbit he used in the act, "that had to be put away, and ether seemed the humane way to do it. So," she went on, "we got a bottle of it," and then later found out "it worked on mosquitoes too." She said, "They fall right over as soon as they come near it." So, going to Brice's Point, "where they don't have mosquitoes, of course, except occasional ones," she brought the ether along, "and of course nothing would suit Mr. El but that *he* had to try it too. So that's why the bottle was out. You rub it on, that's all—and it works."

"Well?" asked Clay after reading.

"That means nothing to you?"

"No, Grace. Not a blessed thing."

"Clay, I never heard of the rabbit—she uses it as a solvent, on her typewriter keys mainly. But also it happens to be the one thing that works on surgical gum—the stuff on adhesive tape. Does *that* mean something to you?"

"You mean if Mr. El—was all smeared up with that gum? From tape being slapped on his mouth? And then was quickly cleaned up——"

"Clay! No more, please!"

"But that's what you mean, isn't it?"

"You must not make me say it!"

"O.K., you don't have to say it, but it's what you mean just the same, and it's been in your mind, or something like it has, from the beginning, when you started your campaign to get me to marry her *now*. You've been scared to death of what's been in her mind, and I can't say that nothing was. But the point is, if something *was* in her mind, it's not there any more! What's been in her mind, that I don't know—she never talked about it to me any more than to you, and God knows I never brought the subject up. But the point is, if anything *was* in her mind, it's not there any more. She's given that idea up. She proved that yesterday when she promised to do as I wanted and break her marriage *up!* This thing now is coincidence—as you'll realize once you think about it. It had to happen sometime! But when it happens *now*, you fit the thing together and come up with adhesive tape—which exists, so far, in your imagination, and your imagination *only!* You're pinning something on her that's completely your own think-up. Do you hear what I say, Grace? You have self-manufactured jitters, *not* caused by what actually happened!"

How much he secretly believed of this impassioned harangue it would be hard to say, but he kept at it, patting her, squeezing her hand, giving her little shakes, as he tried to pull her together. She listened, yielding to his caresses, trying to be convinced, but scarcely abating her woe. Sometimes she interrupted, as once when she spoke about Mrs. Granlund: "I forgot to mention, Clay, that when I spoke to her last night, she said not a word about any plan, any previous plan, to take Elly up to Cape May. And the papers didn't speak of it, either—according to them, Sally was paying him a 'visit.' If she left you to take him from Mr. El and hand him over to Bunny, why didn't Bunny know? And why didn't she tell the police?"

"Maybe—she was just making it simple."

"For the police, perhaps. But how about Bunny?"

" . . . I'm sure she had her reasons."

"That's what I'm afraid of."

They were interrupted by the phone, and he jumped up to answer, hoping for some word. But it was Mankato, Minnesota, calling. Pat, up early, was full of things that had come to him during the night—about Clay, about Grant's, about the Channel City branch. He led off by asking who Clay had in mind to succeed him, and when Clay mentioned Hal Daley, he seemed pleased. "I've had my eye on him too," he said. "He's a fine, resourceful salesman, and our problem, after all, is selling. But, Clay, get to it: name him, make it official, and the sooner you do it, the better. From now on if you try to be half on and half off that job, you'll wind up on the floor. Once the word gets around you're out, then someone else must come in. So, if I were you, I'd call the papers and break it. Then things can go on: he'll know where he's at." Clay said he would do it that day, and Pat went on: "The next thing, Clay, is you. I want you to take some time off—partly because you deserve it and partly to let Hal get started, so he can make his mistakes, deal with the opposition clique, and there's bound to be one, have his brawl with Steven Granlund—all without *you* breathing down his neck. Then, in the early fall we'll say I want you to take the grand tour—drop in on all our branches, spend a couple of days at each, get acquainted with our bunch, and enlarge. See the whole picture, so that when you take over, you'll be president of *all* the company, not just a branch manager reaching up to the ceiling, trying to look tall. It's on us—I want you to entertain, give 'em nice cocktail parties, but that part I needn't coach you on. Now, have I made myself clear? Something you want to ask?"

He was brisk, clear, and a little curt, not sounding at all like a fake. Rather, he talked like the board chairman of a well-established concern, who knew what he wanted and pretty well how to get it. Clay responded in kind, briefly, respectfully, and loyally. When he hung up Grace seemed more composed. "I'll take myself off," she said. "You have big responsibilities—and I have a few, myself. . . . Thanks. I'll keep my fingers crossed. And if things do stand as you think, if it's all a routine affair—it may turn out well after all."

She clung to him, then impulsively kissed him. "Clay," she whispered, "I hope you're right—*but if I can think of it, they can.*"

"Think of what? And who are 'they'?"

"The police."

"Listen: they're not mind readers, *quite.*"

"It's what they're paid for, though. I'm so horribly, utterly terrified. For her sake—and his."

" 'His'?"

"*Elly's!*"

"Oh. Oh, I see."

"My little lamb. He'd be *branded!*"

"Grace! Stop borrowing trouble!"

"Yes, Clay. I'll—try."

It was eleven when he reached the office, and at once he told Hal Daley to "stand by for lunch—I want to talk to you." He drove him to the club, at that hour almost deserted, and they sat at the same table as he had sat at when Pat broke the news to him. He saw Hal give way to the same euphoria as had taken possession of him, and did as Pat had done, talked of small irrelevancies until Hal was himself again. Back at the office, he called *The Pilot*, and they sent over the same reporter that had written the piece about him, flanked by the same photographer. He "released it" for the morning edition, but posted the company notice down on the bulletin board, a battered-looking appendage to the customers' room. As a final rite he ushered Hal into his office, telling him: "The place is yours—I'm out. Except for one personal file, which I'll have sent to my home, I brought nothing in here but my hat."

"Except you don't wear any hat."

Miss Helm sounded waspish, and he realized all of a sudden that she had been in an ill-concealed sulk these last hectic hours and, in fact, of all those who worked in the place, hadn't yet congratulated him. "Hey, wait a minute!" he exclaimed, leaning over her desk and at last twigging the reason. "What's eating on you? Don't you *want* to go to Mankato? The West's prettiest small city? Where Sinclair Lewis wrote *Main Street*? Where——"

"Oh, you mean you're taking me with you?"

"Well, if you want to come, of course!"

Her round, soft, apple-dumpling face wreathed into a smile, and for a moment she was almost beautiful. Then, with desperate self-consciousness: "Don't worry about the file—I'll send it out, Mr. Lockwood! It can go on one of our trucks! It'll be no trouble at all!"

"Then, I'll leave it to you."

But under all this quivered the fear of what was happening to Sally. He ate again in the hotel, to be near the latest editions when they appeared on the lobby newsstand. But the 5:30, when it came out, told him nothing he wanted to know. The police, it seemed, were continuing their investigation, but the body had been released and the funeral set for next day. He went home, called Grace, and found she had heard nothing. Then once more he sat by the window, watching the dark creep in. But, exhausted by strain, by loss of sleep, by excitement, he dozed, and then suddenly awakened. Soft fingers were over his eyes, a loved smell in his nose. "Sally!" he whispered. "*Sally!*"

Then she was in his lap, her arms locked around him, her lips yielding to his. After a long moment he asked: "Is it over? This damned investigation? Or—what?"

"Well, of course it's over! Here I am!"

"I know, but—is there a catch to it?"

"How could there be? He choked on a nut, that's all, as the autopsy plainly showed, with no marks of violence or anything. Their making a federal case of it had nothing to do with that. Clay, they took me down to the beachhouse two o'clock this morning—to talk with MacReady, they said, that nurse the old man had. But I have a different idea. Those cops have great big hearts, and great big hands too, which may have had more to do with it than what Mac-Ready was saying, or the autopsy report, or anything. They told me I could 'retire,' as they called it, but I didn't care to, if you know what I mean. I didn't dare take off my clothes— I haven't had them off since six o'clock last night, when I changed my dress at home and started out for the beach."

"Have you had any supper, Sally?"

"Not much—what I *really* need is a bath."

"Well, we have a bath."

"You going to soap me?"

"Soap you and kiss you and love you."

13

But before the bath came calls that she had to make. The first was to her mother, to whom she explained that she was calling "from some friends' apartment—you know, I gave you their number before." Then she repeated what she'd told Clay, about her release, the autopsy report, and so on. Then she got on to what apparently was the real reason for the call, the question of a dress she could wear to the funeral, "something black and fairly quiet." Apparently Grace had it in stock and would get it to her next day. Then once more, answering questions from the other end of the line, she got back to the day's events, though annoyed at Grace's questions and also at her concern. "Well, Mother," she said sharply, "I don't know why you're upset. His number was up, that was all, from the way he always ate nuts— as who knows better than you? After all, you protested enough, and straight to his face in my hearing, about what could easily happen if he persisted in slapping them into his mouth in that perfectly hoggish way. So, it did happen, that's all." That pretty well wound up this call, and then she rang Bunny, at Cape May, to know "how my lambkin is and how he stood the trip." The lambkin, it seemed, was asleep and had stood the trip fine. She repeated to Bunny what she had said to Clay and then said to her mother, but with more personal details: "It was pretty horrible, Bunny, to go running in there and find him flat on his back, banging his heels on the floor. An old man, dying, is not a pretty sight—I'm still not over *that*."

During all this, Clay changed to T shirt and shorts, put out soap, brush, and towel, and started the water running. At last she fluttered past him, down the hall to the bedroom, and then prettily reappeared, dressed as September Morn, a clean dish towel pinned around her head. She felt the bath with her toe, then climbed in. He soaped her, slowly, carefully, tenderly, and she scrubbed herself with the brush. Then, as the tub filled she stretched out. Occasionally she washed water over her breasts, but mostly she just lay there, her eyes closed, saying nothing. He said nothing, either, being content to drink her in with his eyes as he sat beside the tub on the little bath stool. Presently, though, her face twisted, as though in pain, and she covered it with her hands. "*Now!*" he admonished her, kindly but peremptorily. "No more of that! It's over, that's the main thing! It's all that matters."

"Yes," she said. "It's over."

She opened her eyes, let them wander vacantly. Then, closing them, she recited, in a ritualistic way: "It's over, it's over, it's over—I keep telling myself that. *It's over.*"

Then, in a different voice, opening her eyes again and staring at her hands: "If it is . . . *If* it is!"

"If it is? Of course it is!"

" . . . Clay, I haven't told you all."

"You mean you're going to be held?"

"Well, I hope not—but I could have been. Clay, do you know why they took me? To that beachhouse? At two A.M.? It was to check out a tip from Alec."

"You mean he informed? Against you?"

"Nice, wasn't it?"

"But he wasn't there! How could he know anything?"

"By psychology, Clay—or something. At the hospital he

smelled ether on the corpse and knew the answer at once. I did take the ether——"

"For mosquitoes, the paper said."

"That's right—but as he figured it out, I swabbed the gum off with it from four-inch bandage I used to smother his father to death. So he brought the cops to the house to look for bandage *and* ether. Oh, yes, that's what he did—I could hear him talking to them, a long time, out in the drive. So then, when neither one was found, we had to go down to the beachhouse, to talk with MacReady, they said, that nurse the old man had, but actually to keep up the search. So the ether they found at once, right on the living-room table, where Mr. El had put it—he had to use it, too, and of course smeared on plenty, greedy as he was. All that was proved by his fingerprints right on the bottle. They never found any bandage—though I'll say for them, they looked. All day long their scuba divers were out combing the bay, trying to find it there. Well, who knows where it is? Alec *had* four-inch bandage that he used on wicker baskets, patching them up inside where the sword would cut the strands—so he wouldn't have to buy new ones every week and a half. But that was back in the spring, and who knows what happened to it? The cleaning woman comes, and she could have thrown it out. Or I could have and not remembered about it. Or Elly, God bless him, could have put it somewhere. It wasn't there, that's all we know—but did he have to talk with the cops? Before he talked with me?"

"I wouldn't call it friendly."

"Friendly? *Friendly?*"

She slapped the side of the tub, to indicate how she regarded it, and then after some moments said: "So, that's why this is good-by, Clay."

" . . . Good-by?" he whispered, stunned.

"That's it, much as I hate it."

"But why?"

"Well, Clay, you made yourself clear, and I accept what you said: I come with you now, or don't come. So I can't come with you now, so—good-by."

"But why can't you come with me now?"

"There's something I have to do."

"Yes, but what?"

"Nothing that—concerns you."

"If it concerns you it has to concern me."

After popping herself back and forth, first by pressing a toe to the spigot, then by bumping with her head, she said: "I shouldn't be like this—but it's how I am, and I can't help myself. Clay, when someone does something to me, I can't let it pass, that's all. I have to do something back. And I'm going to. But it may take some little time, and so—I can't come with you now."

She said it with brisk decision, suddenly standing up, tweaking the drain, and starting to towel off. Then, stepping out on the mat and slipping the cloth from her head, she led the way to the living room, still without a stitch on, and curled up in the chair by the window. He followed, tramping around uneasily, trying to readjust to this new development—or old development, now almost in the open. Presently, in a somewhat different tone, she went on: "And there's something I mustn't forget. Clay, in justice to those cops, hands and slobber and all, they didn't really believe him—they did their stuff, of course, but when they didn't find anything, they tried to get through his head I was not the girl he thought. And of course, he had to shut up. But he thought what he thought, and he's not going to unthink it, regardless of what they said, and regardless of time passing by. Twenty years can go by and he'll still think that's what I did—and where do I go from there? Suppose I did come with you. My life would never be safe. And yours wouldn't, darling! I can't forget you for one minute. He could be crazy enough to move against you too—as being in on it, maybe, and helping to raise his boy. He might even move against Elly. I tell you, in some ways he's not all there in the head."

"Who mentioned something like that?"

"You did, Clay. You warned me."

She whispered it reverently, and he went over and kissed her. She pressed his hand and then in a moment went on: "And there's still another angle. Clay, I know you hate it whenever I talk about money, and I glory in you for it. But money figures in this and can't be disregarded. He's a millionaire now—the picture has changed overnight. And from where he sits, to get rid of me he'll have to pay me, plenty. Well? Wouldn't burying me be cheaper? Especially when all it takes is magic."

"Magic? Hey, there are limits to everything!"

"Clay, what do you know about magic?"

"Not much. Just the same——?"

"It's based on illusion, isn't it?"

"I—suppose so. *And?*"

"If he can make hundreds of people think they saw me floating through the air when it's really just a dummy, he can make a dozen think they saw me around the house, after he drove off to work, and before my body was found, curled up in my car, a rubber hose running in from the exhaust. By magic is how it *can* be done!"

"If you mean what I think you mean, they burn you for it in Maryland—and I don't like it one bit."

"Nobody's asking you to."

He had hoped, perhaps, that she didn't mean what he thought, and her answer unsettled him badly, so he didn't speak for some minutes. At last he asked: "*Do you mean to do it by magic?*"

"I'm not a magician, Clay."

"But you must have something in mind."

"Yes—you sit on the porch of a beachhouse, watching

[105

divers at work, looking for stuff to burn you, you think of all kinds of things."

"Then you *do* have something in mind?"

"It's my lookout; it doesn't concern you."

"If I love you, it has to."

"That touches me, but if this is good-by, why do we louse it with stuff that has no meaning? Why can't we have our evening, kiss, and part? I've already told you too much."

"But why *must* this be good-by?"

"You said so! You said it had to be!"

"Sally, *when* did I say such a thing?"

"You said come with you now or—don't come."

"But that was before! We've been all over that!"

"We have, but I can't come with you till—!"

" . . . Yes? Till?"

"I started to say, 'till it's done'—but of course that's out of the question. You're not with it, you don't like it—*Clay, will you leave me alone!*"

She was suddenly emotional, and seemed to be verging on crack-up. He calmed her, then said: "I'm not trying to plague you, Sally—I know the hell you've been through. But I've been through hell, too—and I love you. And I'm entitled to know more than you're telling me."

"Such as what?"

"Such as what you're fixing to do!"

"I've told you it's none of your damned business."

"O.K., we skip that part—just forget it. But I am entitled to know, and it's plenty of my damned business, why this must be the end. Will you kindly explain that to me? If you can?"

"All right, then, I'll try."

She stared out at the stars, breathed deeply a few times, and presently had control. Then: "First of all," she began, "what I have to do, I have to." But "have to" came out *hafta*, sounding much more intense that way. Pausing to let it sink in, she went on: "So, let's suppose it's been done. It was an accident, say the reports, but you have a different idea. O.K., then what?"

" . . . Well, I don't quite know."

"That's why it's good-by."

"Hey, Sally! Not so fast, not so fast!"

"Take your time, Clay. Think it over. *Then what?*"

" . . . You don't *hafta* do this thing!"

"I'm sorry, I do. And I'm *gonna*."

"God, but you make things tough!"

"I'm trying not to. I'm saying good-by."

He walked around in agony, rubbing his hands on his T shirt to dry his damp palms. Then, in a weary, moaning tone, he wailed: "Sally, I may as well tell the truth—we're up tight, why fiddle and foodle and faddle? I could tell myself I couldn't stand for it—I could swear up and down before God I'd never see you again—but two weeks after it happened I'd be calling you up. We've been all over that—I love you! Does that answer you, Sally? I'd break!"

"The question is, would I?"

"Now, what do you mean by *that?*"

"All right, Clay, so it's done. But it won't do itself—*I did it*. Walked into the Valley of the Shadow and then walked out again—as we hope. But then lo and behold, who's there, galumphing up real fast? Why, it's you, chortling in your joy! 'And has thou slain the Jabberwock? Come to my arms, my beamish girl! Oh, frabjous day, calloo, callay'—and whatever the rest of it is! Well, my handsome young friend, when Jabberwocks get slew, someone who just took a walk, who did not even hold the horses, watch for the Bandersnatch, or do *anything* at all for his beamish girl, may not please her as much as she thought he did before. If she's still going to love him, I really couldn't say—all girls are dumb, especially beamish ones, and she could eat her heart out. I wouldn't say she had more sense. But if she hasta, she hasta—and will."

"You're saying I have to help."

"Can't you understand English? I'm saying good-by."

"It's not all you're saying, Sally."

"I know what I'm saying, I think."

"Maybe—but I know the insinuendo."

"Which is, Clay?"

"That I've mock-orange juice in my veins."

"Oh, *that*. I'm glad you brought it up." She reflected, or appeared to, then told him: "I shouldn't have said it, and I apologize. For the rest of what happened that night, perhaps I ought to apologize too, but I don't. When I'm put upon, I have to do something back—I can't help it, it's how I am. I was grievously hurt that night, horribly disappointed—and so I wrecked your place, and ought to regret it, but don't. I'm even *glad*, if you have to know. I might be glad of what I said except that I can't be, and for a very good, simple reason: it wasn't true. You don't have mock-orange juice in your veins or anything like it. You're a fine, upstanding guy, and brave, according to your way of doing. Unfortunately my way of doing is different, and that's what it comes down to. So, I not only apologize for all that I said, but take it back. It was mean and did me no credit. And—I might as well say it all. I don't like saying good-by—I mortally hate it. And my heart will start getting eaten the second I go out that door. So now you know, but what has to be, hasta."

He tramped around some moments, then went to the arch, leaning his elbows on it, and dropping his face in his arms. Then he faced her and said: "I'm in."

"You're— What did you say, Clay?"

"You heard me."

" . . . This room is spinning around."

"You're mistaken. It's standing on its head."

"And things are happening inside of me. Thrills and——!"

"Sally, you do have a scheme?"

"I have—and it's going to work!"

"O.K. What is it?"

"Do we *have* to go into it now?"

She got up and turned on the floor lamp back of her chair, standing before him naked. "Can't we just have our beautiful hour?" she asked softly. But her eyes did not correspond with her voice or, for that matter, with her white, childish loveliness. They were cold, hard, and crafty.

He went over and gathered her into his arms.

"What in the hell has she got you into? Why did you let her do it? Lockwood, she didn't—you did it yourself, single-handed. You're a noble volunteer. And with your eyes open yet—you've known all along what she meant. On top of that, however she fooled the cops, you know she killed that old man. You know everything, and yet you dealt yourself in. So cut out the whats and whys—you are in and that's all that matters. You know you have to have her, and this is the way you get her—and the only way. So get going. So do it. And see that you do it right."

That vanity was his trouble, inflamed by obsessive desire; that his great source of strength, the element in his nature that drove him ahead in business, riding all obstacles down, could also be his weakness; that this giddy twin sister of pride could have a soft underbelly, loving praise above everything else, especially this girl's praise, and dreading her phony scorn—none of this could he have thought of or believed if he had thought of it. To him, it centered on love and a Jabberwock to be slain—a quarry as unreal, as queer, as insubstantial as something in a dream, but a Jabberwock, just the same, to be slain.

14

But having reached his dreadful decision, he entered a new phase, with qualms pushed aside, and no thought in his mind but the deed he intended to do—and, in fact, was as detached about it as he might have been about a campaign to sell meat. By day he talked with Hal, Miss Helm, and Pat, in long phone conversations. By night he drove with Sally, listening as she prattled, as devoid of guilt as he was, of the enormous estate the Gorsuch will had disclosed when filed for probate after the funeral, and of the adventure they had embarked on. Her scheme, as she explained it the next evening they had, was a car crash they would contrive, which would take Mr. Alexis' life but at the same time "look perfectly natural." They could take advantage, she thought, of a quirk in his driving taste, which led him to use an old road, a black-top long since condemned, one of the old original routes from the time of Governor Crothers, which he preferred "for its peace and quiet, as there's no traffic on it, especially in early morning, when he comes home from work." So together they had a look, entering the stretch in question a few miles south of Baltimore, 'at their own risk,' as a big sign informed them. For some distance it ran through meadows that showed green on both sides, being almost on a level with them. But then it began to rise, over a considerable fill, as it passed over a marsh, with water backed up on each side. Then it popped on a bridge, an iron thing over a slough, that rattled and clanked and shook from the weight of the car. Then more marsh, more meadow, and the outskirts of Channel City.

Her idea was a roadblock "that we make by parking the car, at the top of the fill near the bridge, but not a full roadblock, just kind of half-and-half, so instead of stopping dead, he pulls out enough to pass. But the condition that shoulder is in, it could give way under him and spill him down in the water. And so—that would be it." He considered this, parking up near the bridge, examining the fill with a flashlight, and in all ways being thorough. At last he said: "No—it's too risky and has too little chance of succeeding. In the first place, he could stop dead, recognize us, and be warned from then on, so there'd be no way to get him. Or he could pull out and the fill not give way—it doesn't have to, and we can't be sure it will. Or it might give way and he might go down with it, but not till he banged this car, and then we would be in it. Sally, what's basically wrong is it doesn't have *audacity*. It lacks that one thing that could let us win, the means of achieving *surprise*, which is what a thing of this kind *has* to have." She drank all this in, doting, for she detected not a case of cold feet but hardening resolution. But, winding up their evening's work, he observed: "This stretch of road, though, could win for us. Let's work on it, think—see what use we can make of it."

Next night, crossing the bridge southbound, he stopped, and then suddenly cut his lights. When his eyes were used to the dark, he told her: "Something occurred to me: that we could come up on his flank, creep up without being seen, bang our horn, and make him cut his wheel. If surprised, he *has* to cut—it's an instinctive thing—and his regular driving speed will carry him out on the shoulder before he can brake to a stop. It's a matter of two or three feet. *But* we

112]

have to run dark—unless we cut our lights they'll show in his mirror, and surprise will get knocked in the head. And the question is, *Can* we run without lights without landing *ourselves* in the ditch? Well, nothing beats a trial. Are you game?" She whispered she was and he pulled into gear. By that time the stars were brightly visible, as well as various lights, particularly the bright red sign of Chanciteco, as the Channel City Electric Company was called, which glowed in the sky dead ahead. He let in his clutch and started rolling along, while she gripped her arm rest, tense but silently acquiescent. Their progress was bumpy, as the road was full of potholes, especially out toward the side, but they stayed on it, and gradually he increased his speed. Back in civilization again, he pulled over and stopped. "What do you think?" he asked.

"It can be done," she whispered.

"Then, that's how we set it up."

He made his U-turn and started back for another practice run, quickly discovering the thing was impossible northbound, as no pattern of lights would help him. "So what do we care?" he snapped. "Southbound is how he goes, so southbound is how we rehearse." They practiced again and again, until he was fairly confident and could get himself up to forty, "which is average driving speed," he said, "at least on this road." But when she blandly observed, "Then we're set," he cautioned: "Not quite. There's more to it than learning to drive by that sign, and the better we lay it out, the better our chances are. Remember that gang robbing a bank. They take months laying it out—casing the joint, as they call it—running the roads, timing all the details, so nothing is left to chance, and everyone's caught by surprise except them. That's why they're so seldom caught." The next thing, he said, was to find out if without running their lights they could follow a car and then come up beside it. Occasionally cars did appear on the road, and these they began closing in

on, making the pleasing discovery that this feat was somewhat easier than running the road in the dark. "Their lights
show you the way," he whispered to her delightedly.
"There's nothing to it if you're willing to take the chance."
He pulled up beside some of these cars, and she became
greatly excited. "They don't see you!" she told him. "None of
them do—I can tell from the way they drive."

And then one night they pulled up behind a car, a small
blue coupe, and suddenly he whispered: "O.K., I'm going to
pull it—see whether this thing works, here where the bank's
not high and nobody's going to get killed. Watch this guy
now—I can't. I must keep my eye on the road. Watch him
and see what he does."

Driving by the taillight ahead, he ran up close and pulled
left. Then, steering by the other car's headlights, he slipped
up beside it. Then, pressing the horn, he let go a dreadful
blast. The headlights whipped off to one side, then went out.
There came a loud clanking, as of metal banging on metal. A
furious yell cut the dark. He stamped on his brake, stopping,
as the lights' disappearance left him suddenly blind. But in a
moment he started creeping forward and at the bridge put
on his lights. "O.K.," he whispered. "What did he do? What
happened?"

"Went off, that's all."

"Down the bank, you mean?"

"Down on the grass. That's right."

"And? What else?"

"What do you mean, what else?"

"Is he there, or what?"

"Well, do we care?"

"You bet we care—if someone's killed, it's investigated. If
not, it's just one of those things. Is he there? Sally, I asked
you to look!"

"Well, I did look. Yes, he's there!"

"Doing what?"

114]

"Cursing at us! Can't you hear?"

"God, what a help *you* are!"

"You stop godding at me!" And then, as he sniffed at an odor that filled the car. "Yeah, Clay, that's it—you smell something, don't you?"

"Yes, I do. What is it?"

"Adrenaline—from me. Little oversecretion I'm subject to occasionally. Things affect me that way sometimes. Like the bang I got, Clay, when that jerk went down off the road, and I knew it was going to work, this thing we've been fixing up. You'll never know what you did to me. . . . Gives me a funny smell—like a rattlesnake, kind of. Want some nice rattlesnake love?"

"Sally, quit talking like that!"

"Can I help how I feel?"

"Ask how *I* felt, why don't you? I was scared blue."

"Oh, no, Clay, not you!"

"Oh, I was. My mock-orange blood, no doubt."

"Now *you* quit talking like that!"

He talked like that quite volubly, but had no will to resist her, and drove to the apartment, though they had made it a rule these nights to meet out on the street at some prearranged point, she jumping into his car and later jumping out—lest, without knowing it, she was under surveillance.

It was now the middle of August, with the calendar forcing their hand, for not only would Mrs. Granlund shortly return, bringing the child with her, but also the nightclub would change its bill the night after Labor Day, so the victim-to-be would be later starting for home. So they had to make things definite and, when they did, found forced upon them change from the original plan. They had assumed they would do it together, but one night he told her: "If something goes wrong, Sally, and I'm in my car alone, it could still be an accident, couldn't it? A traffic-court case, no worse. But if you're in there with me, nothing can possibly save us. It'll be prima-facie premeditation, and what we get will be plenty. So, I have to go it alone." After studying him and deciding it was not a case of cold feet, she said: "O.K." But that brought up the related question of alibis. "If you're not coming with me," he argued, "then you ought to go further, and fix yourself up with witnesses who can prove you were home all the time and couldn't have been in it at all." She asked about his alibi, and he assured her: "I'll have one, never fear. But my alibi is easier—I live in an apartment house where a switchboard girl is on duty, and all I have to do is have her see me come in, maybe play a scene with her, to fix the date in her mind, and then slip out the back way, so no one knows about it. Of course I'll slip in the back way too when it's over. My problem is simple, if anything ever is. But yours involves people who'll have to swear they saw you that night, at the time when it's to happen. It means, I would say, you have to invite them in and keep them there somehow, so they'll be able to clear you."

She agreed, and they presently set the night for the Monday preceding Labor Day. However, one thing kept gnawing at him, which was Mr. Alexis' driving habits. He knew the Alexis car, having seen it the day of the visit, and she gave him the license number so there could be no mistake. But there was still the question of potholes on the stretch of condemned road, and what Alexis did about them. If, to avoid them, he drove in the middle, the whole thing was in the soup, as Clay knew by that time that he could not pull up from behind on a car driven that way without landing *himself* in the ditch—not a happy prospect. But it was a question of fact, not to be settled by guesswork. So one evening, without telling Sally, he parked near the Harlow Theater, to watch his victim come out and follow him up to work, so he would know. It was around six, and he didn't have long to wait. Mr. Alexis came out the front door, sauntering down the walk, while Sally trotted after him, still in her Portico dress, and backed his car from the garage. Then followed a scene that Clay hated to watch. From up the street came a whistle and then running feet, as eight to a dozen kids trooped up and began dancing up and down. Mr. Alexis, in black tie and Homburg, stared as though in surprise, then took a red ball from his pocket and passed it around. The children examined it closely, bounced it on the sidewalk, and presently handed it back. Mr. Alexis then made motions with it, up and down and crosswise, then gave an exclamation, as two balls were there in his hand. The miracle was greeted with squeals, and he handed the ball back, magnanimously letting them keep it. Then, patting each child on the head, he took lollipops from their ears, causing more squeals, even louder. "Goddam it, don't go soft!" Clay told himself. "You're in this thing, *you're in it!* . . . She could have told me about it, though."

He followed the Alexis car, a big maroon sedan, noting its speed, which stayed at an easy 35. On the stretch of condemned road it picked up a bit, but stayed in the right-hand lane, not veering to the middle. In south Baltimore Clay let it pull ahead, so it reached the Lilac Flamingo first. The club was on Redwood, just off the Little Ginza, which Baltimore calls The Block, and was in a remodeled building, originally perhaps a garage. It had a parking lot at one side, with entrance on Redwood and exit on the cross street. Clay stopped near the exit and, the hour being early, found space for his car at the curb. Mr. Alexis had already parked on the lot, in the space next to the attendant's shack that Sally had said he used. After lighting a cigarette he sauntered to the club, going in by a rear door. But Clay wasn't quite finished yet with his early-evening reconnaissance. There was still the question of Buster and how she affected the plan. Mr. Alexis, according to Sally, always walked her home after winding up at the club, and after visiting with her, walked back to his car for the drive to Channel City, "around two o'clock, as a rule." But it seemed important to Clay, if he were to watch as planned, at the wheel of his parked car, to know all about that walk, especially its direction, so he would know which way to look. So he had looked up Buster in the Baltimore telephone book and now walked to her place, four or five blocks away. It was a small apartment house, with fire escapes showing, on a cross street north of The Block, near Fayette. He started to walk by, then changed his mind, bounded up the stairs, and entered the vestibule. Here, lighting a match, he peered at the names on the mailboxes. Sure enough, the card in one read EDITH CONLON. He blew out his match, stepped down to the sidewalk again, and went on to the corner of Fayette, where he stood for a moment, noting parking conditions, just in case. Then he turned and started back. And then, to his horror, who should come mincing out of the apartment house doorway but Buster, in another sleeveless dress, blue socklets instead of red, and tan shoes instead of white. Her eyes shone with delight when she saw him. "Why, Mr. Lockwood!" she cried.

"Miss Conlon," he said gravely. "How do you do?"

"I told you, call me Buster," she chided him. "Busty Buster, to my friends." Casually, yet with a touch of pride, she bulged the why of her sobriquet, then went on: "But don't worry, I'll keep on calling you Mister—I don't embarrass no one. And yet at the same time I'm surprised at seeing *you* here, in among the ginmills, hotspots, and iniquity dens! For some reason I wouldn't have thought it of you."

"Buster, I sell these pirates meat."

"Oh, that's right, I forgot."

"Their money's as good as anyone's."

"And better in some ways—at least there's plenty of it." And then, leaning close: "Did you see that piece in the paper?"

"I did. Did you see the retraction, Buster?"

"Oh! That was your doing, then?"

"I hope to tell you it was."

He wanted to shake her, yet couldn't quite suppress the smugness of his growl or resist her reaction to it. She was ecstatic in admiration, her "Aw, aw" fairly pulsating with it. Then suddenly she whispered: "Listen!" And then, looking around, noting the passers-by, she pulled him into a doorway, the entrance of a dingy office building, dark in the gathering dusk. Then, mysteriously, her arm around his neck, her mouth pressed close, she breathed: "You know who put it in? The wife, that's who!"

"Oh? You mean Mr. Alexis' wife?"

"He has one. Didn't you hear?"

"Well, I don't know too much about him."

"Oh, a bitch from Bitchenville, Delaware—trying to louse me up. And here's where it gets good: maybe she did. Mr. Lockwood, I could be due for the gate."

"From the—act?"

"Call it that—it's a very nice way to put it. Because things have changed lately. His father died, you know, in a most unfortunate way. By accident, so it was said. But maybe not, if you know what I mean. Maybe he got some help, just the least little push. And is Sonny Boy sore about *that*? Don't make me laugh, Mr. Lockwood. He *was* sore, but then he began to be glad. He's grateful to that dame—look at the dough she made him. *He's* thinking of taking her back. Now, how do you like that?"

"It's a free country, Buster."

"Yeah, for cashew nuts—and all kinds."

She kept studying him, then gave him a pull and pointed. "You see that place?" she asked. "The one I just now came out of? That's where I live, Mr. Lockwood. Why don't you come-up-'n-simmy-some-time?"

He laughed at the Mae West imitation, said: "Well, I'm sure I'd enjoy it at that."

"You might surprise yourself!"

She pulled him back in the murk again, circled his neck again with her arm, whispered: "You're going West, the papers said. You might need someone out there—that calls you Mr. Lockwood—that wouldn't make any trouble—that would kind of look out for you—in a nice little place she would have—where you could relax and have fun."

" . . . I'll think about it, Buster."

"Will you? Sure enough?"

"Did—the overhead stuff get installed?"

"Yeah, but we needn't go into *that!*"

Her manner implied a long story, which was more than he bargained for, so he didn't pursue the subject. Instead, he glanced at his watch, said: "Got to be running along."

"Me too—I'm due at the club. Put on my fish-net tights and handle props for him." Then, with childish pride: "I look good in them!" She lifted her skirt quite high, to show soft, chubby legs, really quite pretty. She laughed when he looked away, put her arms around him again, said: "Listen, I *go* for you! How many times must I say it?"

"I—go for you too, Buster."

"I'm in the book—ring me."

"If I can make it, I'd like that."

"I'm home in the daytime."

"I'll remember."

"And I'm free in the daytime, too."

Suddenly she pulled him to her, gave him a long, wet kiss. He kissed back, not quite knowing why. It seemed the polite thing to do, and was also unexpectedly enjoyable.

"So he thinks he may take her back, and how do you know he won't? How do you know she won't? How do you know anything in connection with this dame? Because maybe you

love her, but the extent to which she can be trusted is scarcely visible to the naked eye. You'd better get it done, get this thing over with—until you do, you're nowhere."

He had raced home, changed, bathed, and doused himself with cologne, to be rid of every last trace of Buster's cloying perfume, in preparation for his 9:30 date with Sally. But the eyes that stared from the mirror were beginning to look a bit wild.

15

Monday, when at last it came, was ushered in by a call from Grace. He had called her once or twice, to keep her "posted," as he said—actually, to keep her from growing suspicious. He had been pleasant enough, saying how busy he'd been, what with Mankato affairs, "and what with Sally's affairs—I may as well tell the truth and own up I hauled in my horns, letting her handle things her own way, as this death changed the picture, in more ways than one, and I can't pretend that it didn't." She had been understanding enough, seeming to believe all he said, and this morning was full of friendly, vibrant enthusiasm. "I just called to tell you," she said, "how happy my daughter is making me and how happy you're making *her*—it must be you, it couldn't be anyone else." She said Sally had asked her to dinner, "tonight, at the house, along with two other women, who live in the same block—it's a hen party, but what she ought to *have!* Clay, I've tried to impress on her that women, to women, are important—that toadying to Bunny Granlund isn't nearly enough. Men decide who's a sexpot—which may or may not be a help. Women decide who's a *lady,* and there's no appeal from their verdict." Clay said that was funny, he had never quite seen it that way, it was an interesting point—and more things, quite as inane, feeling a queer impulse to string the call out—and string it out still more. At last she hung up, he telling her: "Let's keep in touch."

He usually got his own breakfast, but this morning couldn't quite face the chore and so went out to the drugstore two blocks up Kennedy Drive, the druggist greeting him deferentially and keeping him company while he ate. Walking back, he got out the car and drove to the shop, conferring with Hal Daley and stopping to chat with Miss Helm, who was helping out in Accounting. Then it was time for lunch, and he drove to uptown Portico, where Sally was working that day, for a last-minute confab with her. She seated him, had a girl take his order, then came back and stood facing him, as she had the first day they met—though there was no discussion, this time, about the contours of her stomach. "Well?" he asked in a low voice. "Anything?"

"Yes," she answered. "About tonight, and my alibi. I've asked Mother and two other crows to have dinner with me and——"

"They're not crows!" he snapped.

". . . *What?*"

"They're the witnesses on whom your life can depend—so don't start saying crows or even thinking crows. If you're giving them dinner, they have to like your dinner and like you. So——"

"Well, thanks for the lesson in manners!"

"*They're not crows!* Anything else?"

"Yes—in regard to Alec."

"O.K. What about him?"

"I told him, since I'd be up, if he'd skip the visit to Buster and get home in some kind of time, we could talk divorce. So he bit—he's coming straight home as soon as he winds up his show. He'll leave around one o'clock."

"I see. Then—O.K."

"Well, what's the matter, Clay?"

"I said O.K.! . . . Nothing's the matter, except that tonight of all nights, everything *should* be as usual, with nothing to draw attention—"

"Well, if that's all the thanks I get—"

"And I should have been consulted!"

"For trying to make things easy for you!"

"O.K., O.K., O.K.! . . . Anything else?"

For answer she flounced off and then hovered, her figure graceful, her eyes like glittering stones. Once she came up behind him and whispered: "Listen, if you have a case of cold feet—?"

"Do you have a case of cold feet?"

"No, Clay. But——"

"Then quit cracking at me!"

Neither of them, apparently, had meant to quarrel or wanted to, but their tempers were uncontrollably edgy.

He got in his car on the parking lot, then sat fingering the wheel, in thought, and then with a snap of his fingers seemed to remember something. He drove to Washington, parked on the outskirts, near a sidewalk phone booth, got out, and consulted the book inside, thumbing the yellow pages. He drove a few blocks, parked again, and entered a hardware store, buying three cans of white paint with a key to get them open. He drove then to Baltimore, heading south at the outskirts, and on to the stretch of condemned road. On the low part of it, where it passed the meadow, he parked. Then, opening one can of paint, he poured it out on the right-hand shoulder, where it would serve as his marker, to signal his speed-up beside the other car. Going on, he parked again and spilled a second can of paint, this time on the left-hand shoulder, to make a second circular spot, to signal his pull-up to parallel position. Going still further on, he parked again and spilled the third can of paint, so the spot would signal the blast on his horn. Each can, when he had emptied it, he tossed off to the side. When

[125

he drove over the bridge at last, it was well past four o'clock, and after driving around for an hour he arrived at the Chancit Garage, a place not far from home, for the first step in his alibi. "Roy," he said when the manager came over, "I'm just about due, I think, for the works—wash, lube job, tire check, gas—the usual. Will you send over for it? In the morning, maybe?"

"Sure thing, Mr. Lockwood."

"I'll leave it out on the street, give the keys in at the desk—the night girl will put 'em in my box."

"No need, Mr. Lockwood. Your garage knows us and——"

"And I know them, Roy—specially this new bunch they have, with their conscientious ideas. I don't care to be waked up with their nice friendly question about is it O.K., and so on. If you don't mind—"

"Whatever you say, Mr. Lockwood."

"Your man knows the car?"

"But of course!"

"I'll leave it out on Spring Street."

"We'll pick it up, that's for sure."

He drove to the club for dinner.

At nine, after billiards with Mr. Garrett, he parked on Spring Street, locked up, and walked to the Marlborough, taking his mail from Doris, a blonde of uncertain years, a bit washed out, but with more than a trace of good looks. "My, but it's hot out there," he said, glancing at his letters. "You should be thankful for this air conditioning in here."

"Oh, I am!" she said quickly. "It's not really the best, but it helps quite a lot. Even a few degrees is *something*."

"And another thing we can all be thankful for! This is Monday, and a week from today is Labor Day. That breaks the back of summer—then it's the fall of the year!"

"Oh, that's right!" she agreed eagerly. "I've noticed it often myself. After that, life's worth living again!"

He turned to the elevator and then, suddenly, as though just remembering, stopped and fished out his car keys. "Almost forgot," he told her. "Will you put these in my box? In an envelope, if you have one? Mark it *Chancit Garage Will Call.* So Miss Homan knows."

"I will, and I'll leave her a note."

"Thanks, Doris. Good night."

At once, from the apartment, he called Miss Helm at her home. "Will you do something for me?" he asked her. "I have time on my hands now, and I've just taken a notion to do something I've never done—see that beauty contest they have every year down at Atlantic City. I think it's the week after Labor Day, so if you'd take it over—?"

"Why, Mr. Lockwood, I'd be glad to!"

"I'd do it myself, but I have to call Pat Grant, and frankly that exhausts me more than I care to admit—"

"Oh, that I can understand!"

She laughed, and he went on: "I would imagine there'd be less pressure on suites, so if you'll ask for one right at the start, you may get quicker attention." He gave her a half-dozen hotels, as his preferred list, and wound up: "Give me a half hour with Pat and then call me back, will you? Your charges, of course, are on me."

He called Pat, with an idea for precooked picnic hams, "packaged and ready to go, addressed to the teenage trade, and promoted that way. Just an idea, keep it under your hat, but it may turn out we can do something with it." He sat by the window and waited, and presently Miss Helm called, with news that the hotel of his first choice "has a nice suite for you—if you want it, Mr. Lockwood! But hold onto your hat, what it's going to cost!"

"O.K., say it."

"It's forty dollars a day."

"Ouch! But—once in a lifetime!"

"You want me to take it, then?"

"Well, *didn't* you?"

"Well, kind of. But now I'll make it firm."

"Do. And thanks, Miss Helm."

He didn't ask for her charges, but went back in the "office," made out a check for twenty dollars, addressed it to her at home, went out in the hall, and dropped it in the mail slot.

"O.K., you have it all lined up: Chancit will pick up the car in the morning, Doris will remember it's the Monday before Labor Day, the call to Mankato is on record with the time, and Helm's call to you found you home, at a time she'd remember, and perhaps even made note of."

He changed to dark coat, dark slacks, and dark blue shirt, and put on shoes with crepe soles. He studied himself in the mirror, then suddenly turned off the light and caught the sheen of his yellow hair. He rummaged around, found a dark cloth hat. He went to the living room and, without putting on any lights, sat down by the window. His watch said 10:25, and he made himself sit for an hour, being then all but a wreck. But when the time came to leave, he was himself again, acting with quick decision and no slightest sign of fear. He opened the door on a crack, peered out, and on seeing the coast was clear, stepped out into the hall, closing the door quietly. He tiptoed down the hall, the crepe soles making no noise. He didn't bring up the freight car, but opened the door beside it and tiptoed down the stairs. On the ground floor he stepped into the hall again, opened the outside door on a crack. After peeping he stepped out, slipped down the alley, and walked up the street to the car. Unlocking, he got in and drove off, noting he could probably get in later to park in the same spot, for in view of the late hour, no more cars should be due. He used the condemned road, to check on his white spots, finding them easily visible,

128]

even in the dark, when he tried cutting his lights. It was around 12:30 when he pulled up by the Lilac Flamingo lot, and he gave an exclamation of satisfaction at seeing a place to park. He had feared the curb would be full, and it was, almost, but a few feet were clear, and he backed in, pulled up, cut his wheels, and then was snugly parked.

At once he locked up and got out, for another thing he feared was the conscientious policeman having a look around, and sure to be suspicious, at this hour, in this place, of a man in a parked car. He strolled down toward Pratt, stood staring at the ships tied up at their piers, then went strolling back. From the club came bursts of laughter, so he judged the show still went on. Then came a burst of hand-clapping, and he moved to the car, to be ready. Sure enough, after a moment Mr. Alexis came out of the rear door, and a parking attendant, in white smock, popped out of the shack. Mr. Alexis, who was in the same costume he had worn the previous night except for a pink tarboosh in place of the Homburg, handed something over, apparently car keys, and the attendant trotted to the maroon sedan. But then, also from the rear door, there came boiling out a preposterous apparition, in bolero with gold braid along its edges, feathered headdress, fish-net tights, and red shoes. It was Buster, looking pretty, shapely, and cheap, and obviously loaded for bear. "So O.K.!" she screamed at Mr. Alexis! "Go back to her! Who do you think gives a damn?"

Mr. Alexis said something Clay couldn't hear, apparently to calm her down, but without noticeable success. "Divorce! Is that a laugh!" she went on, at the top of her voice. "It's just a come-on, I tell you! She don't mean divorce, she means you!"

But about that time the attendant backed out the car, to the illuminated space in the middle, and Mr. Alexis started for it. But when Buster grabbed him, Clay didn't wait for more. Unlocking, he got in and drove off, heading for the condemned road, and in twenty minutes or so reached it, pulling to one side, stopping, and cutting his lights, but letting his motor run.

There followed a ghastly five minutes while he coughed from compressed excitement, and the car shook a little as the motor grumbled on. Then lights showed in his mirror, and a car shot by. He went into gear, let in his clutch, and raced to catch up. He had barely checked the license when he passed the first white spot, the one on the right-hand side. That meant pull to the left, and he did. Almost at once, it seemed, he passed the second white spot, and that meant pull alongside. He did, but perhaps came up too fast, as it seemed an eternity before the third white spot appeared. He had to wait for it, though, as it was placed where the fill was high enough, the water alongside deep enough, to accomplish what he intended. But at last there it was, and he squeezed down on the horn so it screamed. The lights, like the lights of the blue coupe, whipped crazily off to the right, leaving darkness, so he had to brake. By that time metal was clanking, to a man's despairing yell. Then came a horrible splash, but just before it his heart stopped beating as a woman's scream pierced the night.

He sat in a state of collapse at the realization Buster was in the car, and then his ear caught the whine of a spinning hubcap. He had to have it, he thought, or burn for leaving it there. He jumped out, ran around the car, saw it flashing, and grabbed it while trying not to hear the gurgles of air from the water down below. Then he circled his car, feeling wheel by wheel, to discover which hubcap was missing. But all his hubcaps were in place. In a panic by now, he jumped in with the hubcap, put on his lights, and started. Then his

130]

wits returned, and on the bridge he stopped, pitching the hubcap down in the slough. Then he drove on.

"It's done, goddamit, it's done, no one can ever prove how, so forget it! IT'S DONE, and life can go on! If that poor, sweet little tramp was there in the car with him, that's tough, but you didn't put her there, and life is like that, isn't it? There's nothing you can do now, so forget it, forget it, forget it!"

16

He mumbled that as he drove, but forgetting it turned out easier said than done, and his demoralized state continued all the way home. He found his parking space still clear, but had to battle the car into it, backing, pulling up, cutting his wheels, backing again, pulling up again, until he thought he would scream, before he succeeded in snugging in. Then came the "thirty-nine steps," as he had called them in his anticipation—the walk to the Marlborough alley, on which if he met anyone, or at least someone he knew, it all would go by the board, alibi and everything else, and he might just as well cash his chips. He met no one—on the street, in the alley, on the stairs, or in the hallways, as he pad-padded to his door. At last, inside, he gave a gasp of relief, then raced for the bath, where everything came up, in endless spasms of retching. At last he could rinse out his mouth, go into the bedroom, and undress. He put on pajamas, crept into bed, pulled the covers over his head, and then remembered that one last thing he still had to do. He must put stopples in his ears to account for his failure to answer, in case his phone had rung: "I always use them—they blot out the noise." It had sounded so casual, as rehearsed in his mind, but now merely seemed slick. However, he opened the package he'd bought at the drugstore, mashed a pair in his fingers, and stuffed them in. Saved, in the morning, they would prove he couldn't have heard anything.

In bed again, he tried to think of Sally, to imagine himself with her, and how happy they would be, "once the damned thing has blown over." He couldn't seem to see her. What came to mind was Buster, the sweetish perfume she used, her softness as she unabashedly rubbed against him, and the spittly wetness of her kiss. And when at last he did manage to sleep, what woke him was her scream, all but splitting his ears, and easily going through stopples. In the morning he lay late, but then at last got up, bathed his bloodshot eyes, and after dressing went again to the drugstore, for breakfast. Buying the morning paper there, he found nothing in it at all about the previous night's occurrence, and persuaded himself the car hadn't been found—"may be two or three days before someone spots it, down underneath in that water." But when he paid his check, the noon edition of *The Pilot* was just being rolled off the truck, and he reeled as he saw the headlines, which told how Mr. Alexis was "dead in car mishap," but how "girl alleged foul play." Buying one and reading as he walked home, he learned how Buster, told to jump by her companion, had managed to hurl herself out on the bank, where she lay for some moments unconscious. But what froze the blood in his veins was the brief paragraph that followed:

Under sedation at Channel City Hospital, Miss Conlon was not available for comment, and police refused to confirm or deny that she had observed the license number of the car which forced them off. However, as they promised a statement later, it is believed she did obtain the number, and that when it has been checked out, an arrest may be made.

"So there IS one thing worse than a girl getting killed in that car, and that's a girl NOT getting killed. Boy, are you in

134]

*the soup. You thought that hubcap could burn you, and now
it turns out that it will—it's twenty feet under water, and
still it'll pull the switch. Why the hell couldn't you leave it?
Why did you have to wait till you had it?"*

He called Miss Helm, managed to sound like himself as he
asked her to beg off for him, "with Hal Daley and the rest—
just say I'm taking a day off." She promised to take care of
things for him and he thanked her once more "for what you
did last night." Then he hung up and lay on the bed, slaver-
ing at the mouth and wiping it out with tissues. A long time
went by, and then in midafternoon his phone started to ring.
He let it, but then when it rang a second time and after that
a third, he felt he had to answer. He was startled to hear
Sally, as it had been part of their plan that neither would
ring the other "till everything quiets down." However, she
had been due to ring Buster at three o'clock in the morning
to inquire if Mr. Alexis was there, and then, on learning he
wasn't, to call the police. Now, in spite of himself, Clay was
sharp, telling her: "How many times must I say it? Your
phone could be bugged! From—that other time! You know
what I'm talking about!"

"Clay, I'm not calling from home! I'm in a phone booth
out on the street! Now will you stop yacking at me and
listen?"

"Did you put in the call to Buster?"

"I did, but haven't you seen the papers?"

"Oh, that's right. I forgot."

"Clay, I have to see you."

"Listen, Sally, that's all it needs! I——"

"Damn it, I have to see you!"

"O.K., I'll pick you up and——"

"You will not. I'm coming to you!"

"No, Sally! Please!"

"Clay, today of all days, I can't be hanging around on some street corner waiting for you! They're after me to question me! The cops—and I can't be where they can grab me! I'm coming to you—I'll come in the back way but I'm coming! Now you stay there and wait for me!"

"Suppose the cops come for *me*?"

"It's a chance I have to take—so you hear?"

"O.K., but get it over with!"

He opened the door on a crack, began walking around. In a few minutes it closed, and she was there in the room with him, crisp in a blue summer dress, a little white shell on her head. She didn't offer her mouth, and he made no move to claim it. "Clay," she said quietly, "I hate to say so, but this has to be good-by."

"Has to be? It is. Until we start to fry."

" . . . That's what I came about."

"I'm sorry, but that's the way it's turned out."

"Ah—Clay, I don't intend to fry."

"Have you told the judge about that?"

"Clay, will you listen to me?"

"O.K., shoot."

"*Don't try to drag me in!*"

"*Drag* you in? You *are* in!"

"Oh, no, Clay, not at all. There's not one single, solitary thing to connect me with what you did—with Alec's death—in any way, shape, or form. I can prove I had nothing to do with it—in ways I haven't mentioned to you—all kinds of different ways, which will prove me innocent—which of course I really am. The way *you* messed it up, I certainly can't blame *myself*."

" . . . In what way did I mess it?"

"Leaving that girl to tell tales!"

"I didn't know she was there—had no idea at all. She didn't belong to be there. When I pulled out, she was having a row with him for going off without her!"

"Haven't you read the papers yet?"

"Little. Not all."

"They did have a row, so she told the cops, and she jumped in the car, to be mean. He headed for home, as he planned, telling her she was quite welcome, but her tagging along would cost him a million bucks in the settlement I would ask. So she changed her mind and made it up in the car, and he was to set her down when they got to Channel City and send her home by cab, fish-net tights and all. Then it happened. She says he told her to jump, which she was able to do because part of her meanness was refusing to fasten her seat belt, as he had begged her to do. Oh, she gave the cops an earful, really tore their hearts—including the license number of the car that forced them off. So that would appear to be you. Oh, boy! Messing it up? You——"

"Yeah? And what would *you* have done?"

"What would that gang have done?"

"What gang, for God's sake?"

"The gang, Clay, that you kept talking about? That was going to rob a bank? And planned everything, down to the gnat's heel. They——"

"Would have done *what*?"

"Knocked her in the head, I would think."

"And that's what you'd have done?"

"If it was me or her? You bet it's what I'd have done."

"Sally, I think you're nuts."

"Me nuts? *Me nuts*?"

"I didn't. I wouldn't have."

He repeated: "I didn't know she was there. I did hear her scream, but supposed she went down with the car. But I wouldn't have— I don't do things like that."

[137

"Like *that?* How about killing *Alec?*"

"That was—different."

"How different?"

"Damn it, he was your idea!"

"And so was she—or would have been."

"I couldn't have made myself do it!"

She switched around some moments, not quite so crisp or collected in her movements now, but still under control. "Well," she went on in a moment, "that's all water under the mill. You didn't, that's the main thing, so there's no use talking about it. Do you have it straight, Clay, what I said before? Don't try to drag me in, as it's not going to work at all."

"I have it straight, what you said and what you intend, or think you intend, at least. But now I'll tell you something: if you think, after the way you've stood by me here now after it's done—if you think I'm going to burn and keep my big mouth shut, so you go scot-free and on top of that get the money, you're mistaken. Sally, we had a slip-up, and no one regrets it more than I do. But we were in it together, and that's where we stay, my sweet. You'll burn, you little bitch—because I'll burn you. Now kindly get the hell out."

"No! No! Don't you try!"

"You started this thing! I'll finish it!"

"I didn't start it! You did!"

Control vanished then as she shook him, pleaded with him, and wailed. He said: "Your adrenaline's acting up—excitement seems to affect you. You're beginning to stink, and a rat knows a rattlesnake, baby. So, shove off."

"You son of a bitch. You—"

But she cut off when he grabbed her, took her handbag away, unzipped it, and spilled it out on the table. Spotting his key, he pocketed it, then stuffed tissues, candy mints, handkerchiefs, memos, and the rest of the bag's contents back into it. Then, handing it to her, he said: "Move, or I'm kicking you higher than—"

She went, and he watched her down the hall as she ran to the freight elevator. Then he closed the door.

"Why the hell haven't they come?"

17

He lay down, clenching and unclenching his fists, trying to stop and not being able to. After a while his inside phone rang, and at first he flinched from answering, but then did, whispering to himself: "This is it—they've come, and there's not any hole you can hide in." But it was Johnny, down in the basement, to say his car was back. When he looked at his watch it was five o'clock, and he went down to the street to buy a 5:30. The story was still on Page 1, blown up a little bigger, as it seemed the "mystery deepened" in regard to the motorist who had forced Mr. Alexis off the road. It turned out, however, when he read beyond the headlines, that the "mystery" was mainly in the reporters' minds, as it hinged on the refusal of police to make public Buster's information until they had "checked it out." There was even a separate story on Captain David Walton, with an explanation of his position. "In cases of this kind," he said, "we make it a rule not to give anything out until we give it a check, so innocent people don't get caught in the backwash of what may be a false lead. The trouble is, when someone has been in an accident, especially a bad one at night, and they get a car number, or think they get a car number, maybe they don't get it right, and for us to make public that number before we checked it out could just mean a barrel of trouble. Don't worry, this looks just as fishy to us as it does to anyone else, but we don't go off half-cocked."

Back at the Marlborough, instead of going in through the lobby, he walked down the ramp to the basement, ostensibly to pick up his bill, which was tucked under the wiper, actually to talk with Johnny, as to the police, and whether they'd been around. He didn't exactly know what "checking out" consisted of, but it seemed to mean an investigation of the car's whereabouts at the time the accident occurred. He let himself notice a dent in his fender, a small thing the size of a quarter, that had been there some time, gave an exclamation of annoyance. "I meant to tell Roy about that, have him take it out—and forgot it. Did they ask about it, Johnny, or say anything at all when they brought the car back?" Not to him, said Johnny, not taking a great deal of interest. It was just such a lead as should have smoked Johnny out, inevitably start him talking, in case others, such as police, had done any asking that day. But Johnny didn't respond, and so far as Clay could detect, no guile was in his face, such as must have been there if police had been around and enjoined him to silence. Baffled, Clay had to conclude that no check-out had yet been made, at least here, where the car was usually stored. He went up by the freight elevator, called Roy at Chancit. It seemed Roy had noticed the dent and had meant to drop him a note, along with the bill, and then kind of forgot it. It was no job to take out, he said— they could suage it and spot in the paint with no trouble. The whole thing would amount to less than ten dollars. Clay listened, giving plenty of openings to mention police if they had been around. Roy didn't take the bait.

Bewildered by now, Clay went in the kitchen, opened a can of beans, and while swallowing them down finished reading the paper, especially the story on Buster, which he hadn't got to yet, as the one on Captain Walton had seemed much more important. A picture of her, in shapeless hospital attire, with an inset of her in tights, and another of Mr. Alexis, made a Page 1 layout, and under it was an interview, in which she made "veiled hints" as to the guilty motorist's identity. "What's all this checking out?" she had demanded of the reporter. "I gave them the number, didn't I? They've had time to look it up. They know who it was and, brother, so do I. Why don't they make an arrest? What are they waiting for?" It was a costly interview, as she was to find out later, but to Clay it was incomprehensible, as it didn't at all match up with what he thought she should feel if she did know who it was. To her, he was surely a friend, and her reaction must have been shock, coupled with hurt. But the emotion she seemed to show here was of malice compounded with hoped-for revenge, or perhaps of suspicion that hoped for proof. Most perplexing of all, she voiced no surprise at what had been done, but seemed almost to regard it as something expected. He washed up his plate, went to the living room, and sat looking out on the stars, "perhaps for the last time," as he glumly told himself, still grinding the riddle. His outside phone rang and he sat there. It rang a number of times, and he made no move toward it. But around nine, when Doris rang from downstairs, he grimly got up and answered, sure "they" had come at last. "Lady to see you," said Doris. "The same one, Mrs. Simone—hey, she's quite a looker."

"Send her up," he said.

But the receiver was hardly in place before it flashed through his mind how horrible it was going to be if Grace was there with him when they finally came, and not only witnessed his arrest but also learned the reason for it. He grabbed up the phone again, batting at the bar. "Doris!" he barked. "Is she still there? Hold her—don't let her come up. Tell her I'll be down!"

She was in a blue summer dress, with her usual crimson accessories, and he grabbed her hand, almost clinging to her. "My, but I'm glad to see you!" he exclaimed. "But won't you

[143

ask me over? If we go upstairs, it'll be nothing but calls from Mankato, with the local bunch dropping in—you've no idea what it's like, being president-elect of a big meat corporation."

"I'd love to ask you over."

They took another stroll through the night, with more pauses to stop, look, and listen. Like most artists, she took a profound interest in natural phenomena, the day, the night, the seasons, and all that these things produced. This time they stared at early chrysanthemums and listened to the crickets, "a sure sign of fall," as she said. The lightning bugs enchanted her. "They give light without heat," she whispered, "the way you do with paint."

In her apartment, after turning on lights, she took off her hat and gloves and put out a highball tray, with glasses, ice, fizz water, and Scotch, while he watched her, as always, in delight at her graceful form and simple, quiet elegance. Then from a closet she got out his picture, now finished and framed—and set it up on a chair. It showed him lounging in the maroon coat she had chosen, his golden hair aglint, his blue eyes on the beholder. " . . . Well?" she asked. "Do you like it?"

"Yeah, but it's too damned pretty."

"How, too pretty?"

"It's too—*idealistic!*"

"It's not!" Indignantly she faced him. "Clay Lockwood, you don't know yourself, that's your trouble—*always.* You are idealistic, and sometimes it shows in your eyes—the way it did the first night we met, when you talked about Tom Lea, and Mexico, and why they fought their war. I didn't know much about it, but I could feel what it meant to *you.* And that's what I wanted to catch. I couldn't. And then that morning I did—that Sunday morning when I finished it. The knife did it, I didn't. And suddenly it was there, what I'd been trying to get. And now you don't like it!"

"I'd love it—if I believed it."

"Well? Can't I *make* you?"

"I'd give anything if you would!"

He hadn't expected the fervor in his voice, and she looked at him quite strangely. "At least," she said, "I imagine they'll hang it—in their board room, I mean."

His mind formed the words, "If they *ever* hang it," and for a moment nostalgia claimed him, for all that might have been except for his monstrous folly. But he didn't say them, and began a digression about her painting, noting its "vigor." But even while he talked he knew he was filling in time, stretching things out to delay his return home, to face what he feared would be waiting there. But when she chimed in, encouraging his loquacity, he knew she was doing the same, and had been, with all her talk about mums, crickets, and lightning bugs. Abruptly he cut in and asked: "What did you want of me, Grace? Neither of us has opened our mouths yet about what's on both of our minds."

" . . . Clay, I'm almost ashamed to say."

"Something's riding you."

"Yes, and I had to come to you, Clay, as you're the one person on earth who can possibly understand why I feel as I do."

"About this death, you mean?"

"Yes, Clay—this death."

"Grace, it's natural that you'd be upset."

She stared at him, clutched him, buried her face in his coat, and whispered: *"I'm not—that's why I'm so ashamed!"*

" . . . Wait a minute. Talk plainer."

"Clay, you know what I feared?"

"What I *said* you feared."

"That's right—you never made me admit it, and I'm grateful to you for that. But that's what it was, just the same, a horrible, haunting nightmare that wouldn't go away. Well, last night it happened, in a natural way—or at least accidentally. It's as though I've been filled with gas and am going to float away. It's—such a relief! Clay, instead of grieving for a boy who was nice to me, who treated me *so* well, who was *everything* any mother-in-law could *ask*, I'm happy it happened this way! It's a horrible thing to admit—I can't help it! I try not to be glad and I am! But at least you'll understand why. You know it's not something I just now thought up, that popped into my mind. It didn't—it's been there. Ever since—one day when her eyes told me."

"O.K., talk it out."

"I have. That's all, Clay."

"Then, take it easy. Try to relax."

He put his arm around her, pulling her to him, wiping her tears with his handkerchief, holding it to her nose, saying, "Blow." She blew, and he kissed her and pressed her and patted her. She said: "It's not all! I'm not sure you still understand! It's not on my account that I feel this way—or even on hers mainly. She's my baby, I'll always love her. But mainly it's for *him!* My little grandson, Elly! Alec's little boy! Perhaps if Alec can understand that, wherever he is—he'll forgive me, Clay!"

"But, Grace, you haven't done anything!"

"Oh, but I have. In my heart I've done plenty!"

She gained control a little, but it increased her compulsion to talk. "Clay," she wailed, "you'll never know, *no one* can ever know, the nights I spent—imagining myself with Elly—holding him on my lap—while we waited for word—the flash that might come from Annapolis: her sentence had been commuted, so she wouldn't have to die! And even worse, the days I spent with him—when her sentence *was* commuted—driving up to the prison, the Maryland penitentiary, for the monthly allotted visit. Clay, I've been to that penitentiary: Fisher's, one year, bid on the uniforms, and I did the design. I had to talk with the warden and went there. I guess it's all right, clean and humanely run—but,

Clay, a prison's a prison, and any prison is horrible to me. The picture of her there, talking to him through the wire, would make me actually *ill*—and that he'd spend the rest of his life with that scar, that brand, that mark of shame, was more than I could bear. So, knowing what I went through, perhaps you'll understand—"

"Is that all?"

"I'll try to stop talking about it."

Intermittently, what seemed to her a dream out of the past now began looming to him as reality in the future, and his voice husked as he spoke. In an effort to change the subject, she drew a long breath and said: "The funny thing is that *she* seems to take it just opposite. I wouldn't have thought Alec meant much to her, but she's taking it very hard. And incidentally, Clay, it would be in terrible taste for you to go to her now, but you *could* call her up—I *hope* you have already."

"I saw her, as a matter of fact."

" . . . You've seen Sally? Since it happened?"

"She came over. We—had a disagreement."

"Disagreement, Clay? What about?"

"I wouldn't feel free to say."

"You picked a quarrel? At a time like this?"

"I didn't, Grace. She did." Then, gravely, he added: "She said it was over between us, and this time I'm sure it is."

"Well, you don't seem much upset."

"Upset? I'm—thrilled."

Indeed, as he spoke he knew his feeling for Sally was gone—whether from the fear that froze his blood, or disgust at the way she had smelled, or resentment at her ratting, he didn't know and couldn't seem to care. Grace stared a few moments, and then wonderingly said: "I honestly think it's true. You don't sound the way you did before when you'd swear up and down it was over."

"She means nothing to me at all."

Grace, a little calmer now, thought this over at length, then reflected: "There'll come times when you torch for her—in that, you'd only be human. And yet, perhaps it's just as well. If you're not free to say what she quarreled about, I'm not free to ask, and I don't. Quite possibly, though, in back of the reason she gave, another reason lurked, that she probably didn't give, and wouldn't admit, even to herself. She's my flesh and blood, and I love her, but she has a selfish streak. Very possibly now that she *has* the money, that huge Gorsuch fortune, she got speedy second thoughts on sharing it, even with you. So, it could be you're just as well off. And if that sounds strange, after my egging you on, all the promoting I did, I can only say the *reason* I egged you on doesn't exist any more. As I explained—oh, blessed relief! So, perhaps you should thank her, Clay."

"One way to look at it, certainly."

"Not that it's been any bed of roses for *her*. Especially this show the police have put on. Why, you'd think hers was the car that Buster saw last night, the questions they've asked everyone!"

" . . . When was all this, Grace?"

"Tonight. All evening."

"And—who is 'everyone'? Who did they question?"

"Me, for one. They were here. And those other two women, too. That came to dinner last night. At Sally's."

"And what did they want to know?"

"Where she was last night. What she was doing. Where her car was. Fortunately all three of us knew it was in the drive. We helped carry things in that Sally'd brought home for supper. But— Clay, is anything wrong?"

"No! It seems strange, that's all."

"Strange? It seems weird!"

Little heat lightnings of hope began shooting through him as he began fitting all this to the bafflement he had felt

148]

about the failure to check out his car. And then suddenly, in one blinding flash, hope blazed into certainty. The phone rang, and when Grace talked, it was obviously to Sally. Quickly, tensely, she kept saying: "Yes! . . . Yes! . . . Yes, of course, darling"—and then suddenly hung up. Whisking the painting into the closet she had taken it from, she said as she locked it up: "Clay, you'll have to go now. Sally's on her way over. That's what it was, all right—that little viper gave in Sally's number, believe it or not. The reporters are there now, and she must get away from them somehow—I told her to come here. So—I'm sorry, but this is no time to tell her what's between you and me!"

"Certainly not—I'm on my way!"

"And thanks! You've been wonderful, Clay!"

"Kiss me?"

"Now that I can—without any sense of guilt!"

His heart sang. Out on the street, he hummed as he started home and then changed his mind and crossed to Rosemary Park, where he sat on a bench and waited. In a few minutes Sally drove up and, after parking, got out, an overnight bag in her hand. She looked up and down the street, making sure she wasn't followed, and then went in. He looked at his watch, found it was after twelve, and instead of going home headed downtown and walked to the Chinquapin-Plaza. Here he sat for an hour in the lobby until a bellboy came in with a bundle of morning papers. Several others besides Clay came forward to buy as the boy cut them open and put them on sale. With his, Clay went back to his chair and read every word that was there. It appeared that "though police still refused to talk," it had become known through other sources that the number Miss Conlon had seen last night was the same as that borne by the "second Alexis car," the one usually driven by Mrs. Alexis. The writing was indirect, a masterpiece of left-handed insinuation, and Clay was some time twigging that the reason for it was libel—the paper dared not accuse Sally directly. But the implication was plain, and when he had read to the end, he got up and walked home, his heels lifting in a queer, uncontrolled way. He reached the Marlborough around two, waved at Frank, and went up. In the apartment at last, he was suddenly consumed with hunger, and broiled a Grant steak. With it he had peas and boiled potatoes, which he got out of cans and heated. For dessert he had apple pie and with that had champagne, walking around with his glass and guzzling it as he went. The bubbles tickled his throat and he started to laugh. He laughed and laughed and laughed.

"Boy, is that a joke, is that one for the book! Maybe Buster had the wrong pew, but was she in the right church. And the beautiful part is, your alibi is not only airtight, but snake-proof, one hundred percent. You have the phone calls, and not only them but the garage bill, to prove you never went out of this place. If she says different, it's malice. But what the hell? She won't open her mouth—she dare not. To drag you in, she has to drag in herself. You're in the clear—and she's not. Is that a laugh? Is it funny or isn't it?"

18

The next two or three days passed as though in a dream, the happy, sun-flecked dream that follows a dreadful nightmare. He called the shop each day, going through all the motions of a sharp president-elect; he lunched at the Chinquapin-Plaza, greeting many friends; he dined at the club, playing billiards with Mr. Garrett; he called Grace a number of times, noting her kittenish manner and wanting to see her. He read the papers, all editions, and was just a bit upset at the ease with which Sally proved her alibi, as this somewhat dampened the joke. But the funeral restored his spirits, as Buster showed up in deep mourning, her picture getting more space than Sally's. And when Sally beat a retreat, drove off to Cape May in her car to visit Mrs. Granlund and rejoin her little son, he read and reread the item, being able to laugh again. And then one morning Miss Helm called from the shop to say Miss Conlon was there—"you know, that girl Buster that was here with Mr. Alexis and got hurt when he was killed." It seemed that "she wants to see you, Mr. Lockwood—but if you want to see *her*, that's what I thought I'd better find out. She looks better than she did— at least she's decently dressed. But—! Sir, do you want me to head her off or—what?"

"Tell her to come, Miss Helm."

"Oh?" said Miss Helm, startled. "You want to see her?"

"I don't want to. I feel I should."

"Then O.K."

And, indeed, the girl who stepped from the elevator *was* different, not only in dress but also in manner, from the one who had hung on the rail, dangling her heels and kicking them. She was in black, a crepe outfit with black hat, bag, shoes, and gloves, that slimmed her curves quite a lot, without at all concealing them. She seemed glad to see him and grateful that he should see her, but her manner was reserved, and she made no such overtures as she had the last time they met, on the street up in Baltimore. Once in the apartment, she took the chair he offered, saying, "Oh, I'm all right," to his somewhat nervous "How are you?" and then sat silently drawing off her gloves. Then, drawing a long breath: "*So*, Mr. Lockwood, I won't take up any more of your time than I absolutely have to, but so you'll understand what I've come *about*, I'll put it on the line, why I *had* to come. Mr. Lockwood, that woman's out to get me."

" . . . What woman, Miss Conlon?"

"I told you, call me Buster."

"Yes, Buster. Who are you talking about?"

"Her. Sally. That—Mrs. Alexis."

"Oh." He tried to ponder this, to get its full implication, but his mind was blank. Then: "In what way, get you?" he asked.

"She's trying to say I did it—killed Alec!"

"That you killed him? How could you have?"

"By grabbing the wheel or something—twisting it."

"Buster, that makes no sense!"

"I didn't say it did."

"But what makes you think she's trying to?"

"I don't think, I *know!* She called and told me so, right on my hospital phone! That she would get me if it was the last thing she did on earth, for what I did to her—giving her number in! When I saw it! Right in front of my eyes!"

"But the papers said that her car——"

"Was home! So she said, and her mother, and her friends. But I know what I saw, don't I?"

She gave an impassioned account of the accident, especially her companion's heroism in pushing her out to safety, though held himself by his seat belt. She wound up: "What brought me to, lying there on the bank, was a sound, of a car door being shut, and I made myself open my eyes. At that moment lights came on, and her number was looking at me."

"But, Buster, wait a minute. At a time like that, there's such a thing as hallucination—people *think* they see things that they *don't* see!"

"And prevarication, as the cops are trying to say."

"And— What was that, Buster?"

"They're making a thing of it, that I knew whose number it was *before* they gave it out! O.K., maybe that was dumb, talking to those reporters there in the hospital room, and saying I already *knew* who the number belonged to. Well, I ought to know, oughtn't I? I picked up her plates for her when he asked me to, and she was too shiftless to do it—last March this was, and I stood in line at the Department of Motor Vehicles. What's the big deal in *that?* I saw her number, I tell you! There in the dark of the night!"

On this subject she was obviously somewhat unbalanced, and he didn't pursue it further. Uneasily he asked: "O.K., but where do I come in?"

"In regard to the number, you don't."

She opened her bag and took out a paper, an insurance policy, he saw. Handing it over, she said: "This he took out for me, couple of years ago—could have been three, I'm not sure. It's life insurance, Mr. Lockwood, but a special kind, that's cheap. Term insurance it's called, and the idea of it was I would be protected, if something happened to him, until his father would die, and he would come into the money, so a new deal would come. He could settle with *her*, marry me, and not need this kind of insurance. So his father did die, with some help from her, as he thought, like I told you the other night—and a new deal came indeed. Because believe it or not, he turned around and became grateful for what she did—he began to wonder, Mr. Lockwood, if taking her back wasn't cheaper than making a settlement. At least *I* got that idea! Well, I said so before, didn't I? So that's what the row was about, out on the parking lot. But how this thing comes in, this policy you have in your hands: he meant to let it lapse, as it had no point any more. The premium's due in October, and she's trying to make out I had until then to kill him if I was going to cash in. *She* says I made him go up the ladder to check the stuff in the Lilac, the overhead rails they put in, so he'd fall and break his neck. So he did go up and he fell, but he didn't break his neck. An electrician caught him, and no harm was done. But then she says, when that didn't work, I went with him on that ride and——"

"Wait a minute! How do you know she says that?"

"Didn't you hear me? She told me so!"

"Over the phone? She said *that?*"

"She screamed at me a half hour, until I really had to wonder if she wasn't off her nut."

" . . . O.K. And I?"

"It would help me if I could refer them to you, and you'd say you were the one, not I, who told him he had to climb up. And make sure those rails were level."

"The police? Of course refer them to me."

"You remember telling him that?"

"I certainly do. You can count on me to the limit."

She thanked him, started pulling on her gloves. But he had opened the policy and now started reading it. And then suddenly he exclaimed: "But this thing is in *force!* You stand to collect twenty-five thousand bucks."

"That's right—if I put in my claim."

"*If* you put it in? You'd *better* put it in! *Not* putting it in would be tantamount to admitting you had some reason *not* to." And then, suddenly rattled and licking his lips: "Or at least so I would think. Unfortunately I don't know—neither one of us knows. Buster, what you need is a lawyer."

"Oh, sure—I'll get one, right away." Her tone was ironical, and she continued pulling on the gloves.

"Hold everything."

Every place has its ace criminal lawyer, and Channel City's was Nat Pender, whom Clay knew pleasantly enough, as a fellow club member. He rang him now and, after recalling himself, said: "Nat, a friend of mine's in trouble, and I'm wondering if I can send her to you."

"Why, I think so. Who is she?"

"Name's Buster Conlon—that girl who——"

"Oh, yeah, the one that was with Alexis. Say, she *is* in trouble, Clay—it could be, unless something is done. According to my grapevine, there's an insurance angle and——"

"Yes, that's why I called you, Nat."

"Well, then, if you'll have her come in—?"

"This afternoon, maybe?"

"Yes, but let me look at my book."

"O.K., Nat, but first things first, and before you do any looking, what's this going to cost? I mean, as a down payment, like?"

"Clay, with you I'd hardly ask——"

"Nat, I'm no different than anyone else."

They backed and filled through the immemorial *politesse,* but presently Mr. Pender admitted that "in a case of this kind, where she's not actually charged and it's mainly a question of getting the cops off her back, I let you off light—I feel it rates a thousand-dollar retainer, but I don't take your shirt. That comes later."

"She'll have the check in her hand. Now look at your book and let's set it up—what she does and what you do."

When Mr. Pender had looked at his book, his manner was somewhat different, he obviously meaning to give value for value received. He said: "Clay, I have an hour I can give her, by shifting some things around, if she'll be here promptly at two. And what I'll do is have my girl call headquarters and leave word for the men assigned to this case that if they want to talk to her then, she'll be here to answer their questions—in my presence, and I'll decide which ones. But, Clay, for your information, and so she cooperates, I've found it's smart at this stage of the game to have her answer them *all*. They know, as they've dealt with me many and many's the time, that after that she clams—they'll have to come to me. That brings on a new phase. But I've also found that it's smart to have the reporters come, so after the cops are done they have a go at her, and perhaps are given a statement. Then, Clay, I hope you get the point: That's it! Unless she's charged, there isn't any more, because they can't stay on her back and just twiddle their thumbs. Do you get it, Clay? And will you explain it to her? So she doesn't think I'm playing the deuces wild? When it's not bottled up any more, it can't explode in her face!"

"I do get it, and I'll see that she does."

Going down the hall to the "office," he wrote the $1,000 check and put it in an envelope, which he marked: "Mr. Pender, Kindness of Miss Conlon." Then he sealed it and went back to the living room, where he sat down with her and explained Mr. Pender's plan. She seemed to get the point, and then he handed over the envelope, telling her: "First of all, give this to Mr. Pender."

She took it, glanced at it, said: "You're supposed to leave it open when you say 'Kindness of Miss Conlon.' Sealing it's not polite."

"Unless Miss Conlon is nosy."

"How much is this check, Mr. Lockwood?"

"It—sweetens the pot, that's all."

"I want to know. If I do make a claim and it's paid, I can pay you back—and I want to. Now say: How much?"

"Buster, you mind your own business."

She came over and sat in his lap, patting his cheek and kissing him. "You don't know what it means," she whispered, "having a friend like you."

"I don't like it, you being kicked around."

"Mr. Lockwood, you make me want to cry."

"Now! There's nothing to cry about!"

"Oh, yes, there is. We've been so busy, talking them first things first, I haven't told you all. If things *should* start breaking for me, thanks to you, Mr. Lockwood, it would be heaven right on this earth. Like if I get the money, I could do things for my folks, up in Havre de Grace, like taking the mortgage up that's hanging over their heads. And I got job offers too, now that my picture's been in and everyone's talking about me—even Mike will put me on. I used to strip, Mr. Lockwood, and I can go back to that trade. If I do say it myself, I look good in my G string. Wait! I'll show you—"

"No, please! Not now, and not here!"

"O.K., but when I start ecdizzying around— Mr. Lockwood, there's a word and a half, ecdysiast. Who invented that? Do you know?"

"Mr. Mencken, I think."

"Who's he?"

"Writer. Dead now."

"Well, he did something for our business. Because you play around with it, it's a laugh—oh, I've used it often. Two of them, specially—you leave off the T and——"

"Never mind, I can imagine!"

"It comes out——"

"No!"

"Funny!"

She laughed as she flirted with him, playful as a puppy. But then suddenly she wrapped an arm on his head, held his face up to hers, and said: "I'm making it up to you—this check you wrote, I mean. But there's one thing I'd like understood: I loved that guy—Alec, I'm talking about. Maybe I wasn't a saint, the way I treated him, but in my heart I loved him. And he loved me, Mr. Lockwood. O.K., the money was there, and sometimes it went to his head, so foolish ideas got in it. But he loved me. Well? What do you call that? Pushing me out that night—"

"Greater love hath no man—!"

"That's right! And he did lay down his life!" She waited a long moment, then reverently whispered: "For me!"

" . . . Are we done?"

"Did you hear me? I'll make it up to you."

"Thanks, Buster."

"You want me to call?"

"Well, why don't I ring you?"

"I mean, today? Tell you how I make out?"

"Oh, by all means! Please!"

"Well, on that other—of course you have to call me."

"O.K., we'll leave it like that."

At last he got her out and shortly after went out to lunch, eating in the drugstore. Then he came back and began marching around, looking at his watch, drying his hands on his handkerchief. Around three, when his phone rang, he jumped for it. "Clay?" said Mr. Pender. "It's all over—the boys did their stuff, police, reporters, and a faceless silent guy that looked like an adjuster. She's in the clear—they really had nothing on her. The insurance, of course, would be bad, back to back with something else, but when nothing else was there, it didn't mean a thing. So she's happy as a lark, having a bath in mud. She's putting her claim in and is going to collect, I think. And next week she goes to work for

Mike Dominick, in a show he's putting together to take the place of the magic—ecdizzying, she calls it, and I'm sure it's going to be dizzy."

But Clay's conscience stirred, he not wanting Buster to bear any part of the cost his act had caused her. He said: "Swell, Nat—you've covered yourself with glory. But what's the tab? On that claim. What are you charging her?"

"Oh, I have nothing to do with that."

"I thought you'd taken it over."

"She doesn't need a lawyer, may be better off without one. Of course if there's trouble about it, then I'll step in, of course. But so far it's her affair, and you're all paid up, boy. If that's what you're worrying about."

"As a matter of fact, it is."

"I'm paid in full, Clay. And thanks."

"Hey, I bet that's ethics."

"It's good for the grass, makes it grow."

He had hardly hung up when the phone rang again, and this time Buster gave her account, at somewhat greater length, but even more cheerfully. He gave his congratulations and listened to more of her thanks. She wound up: "I'll be waiting for your call."

"I'll look forward to it, Buster."

"I'll make it up to you. Nice."

"O.K., she's a sweet, harmless thing, and you clobbered that snake but good. All's well that ends well, and now get on with your life."

19

He got on with his life by asking Grace to dinner and taking her to the club, the first time she had ever been there. She was still in her mood of elation, though resentful of "that girl—why, the nerve of her, showing up as she did at the funeral, and after accusing Sally." To his mouth came a hot retort, but he caught himself in time and said mildly: "Oh, well, it's been a dreadful time for everyone, and for her too, no doubt. At least she mourned him—she was sorry he was dead, which was more than Sally could say." It was more than Grace could say, as she had already confessed, in bitter shame—which may have been why she changed the subject to the blue haze on the water. "Do you see how it blots out the shoreline, on the other side of the bay, so everything seems suspended between heaven and earth, day and night, yesterday and tomorrow, in kind of a smoke-blue Nirvana?" But Nirvana got a jolt when three children fetched up against her, all in bathing suits, and a mother called out her apologies. Indeed, the place swarmed with children, and he apologized too. "It's the pram race they had today," he explained, "but if it isn't one thing, it's another. It goes on all summer this way, but I assure you that after Labor Day it's a wholly different place."

When he said "Labor Day," he remembered, all of a sudden, what he had quite forgotten: the hotel reservation he had, the one Miss Helm had got him, the following week in Atlantic City. It seemed like a thing from another century, but he had it, just the same, and in a moment he said: "Grace, forget the kids. Speaking of Labor Day, I happen to think of something else. Pat Grant kept after me to go somewhere and relax, so they have this beauty contest down at Atlantic City, and I thought: 'Once in a lifetime, why not?' So I'm reserved. I have a sure-enough suite—sitting room, bedroom, and bath—forty dollars a day. How'd you like to share it with me?"

" . . . Are you propositioning me?"

"Well, you're pretty enough. Yes, I am."

"Oh! Oh! Oh! Get thee behind me, *please!*"

"You sound almost as though tempted."

"Tempted? I'm practically a gone duck!"

"O.K., then, it's a date?"

"I didn't say so. Not—yet."

Thoughtfully she ate her crab soup and after some minutes went on: "Clay, I never concealed from you how you made me feel, even that first night. That first—*evening.* 'Night' sounds so damned intimate—no doubt I betray myself. Well, I owned up, didn't I? And I might have landed you, have stolen you away, even from luscious Sal, *if* I had made the *try.* I couldn't, I was bound. By—what I felt I must do, the campaign I had to start. But you know what it was, we've been all over *that.* Now, however, that's changed. The main thing holding me back, as I said the other night, doesn't exist any more—Alec's dead, and I don't have to fear for him the way I once did. And *she* seems, the way she talks, just as cold on you as you seem to be on her. So, I'm out of my vows! I'm free—to work my wiles on you."

"Then, you're going?"

"Well—I didn't quite say that."

"Listen, make up your mind: yes or no?"

"Clay, I have made up my mind. Darling, it's yes—with

beating heart and head all full of thoughts. *If, as, and when*
you up your offer."

"How can a proposition be upped?"

"It can be done if you try."

She looked at him with heavy-lidded eyes, her mouth
puckered a bit, for some time. Suddenly he knew what she
meant. He looked away, took in the wholesome scene of
childhood slapping around half bare; of motherhood sipping
martinis; of fatherhood smoking cigars; of the smoke-blue
Nirvana tinting the sunset with peace. Then a hunger pos-
sessed him, for wholesome, clean things, and he reached out
a friendly finger to touch the back of her hand. "O.K.," he
said, his eyes growing soft, "I get the point: a proposition is
upped when you make a proposal out of it. So consider it
upped. But—you made your little speech. Now I'd like to
make you one."

He thought, then went on: "I never concealed from *you*
how I felt that evening. You have to admit I made passes
from the start—whatever they are. I've never quite known,
really, but whatever they are, I made 'em, at you, and meant
'em. So, our stars weren't in conjunction, and nothing came
of it then. But I knew who was good for me, who the deepest
part of me wanted, who the best part of me wanted. And
that's why, when we both were going through hell, you
because you were decent, I because I wasn't, at least for a
while, that same part of me wanted you and thought of
nothing else. Then I woke up. The lightning struck and
opened my eyes, so at last I was free too—of my vows, or
insanity, or whatever it was. So I hereby up my proposition,
from wanting to, and with no regrets at all—especially for
anyone else. I propositioned you, with all kinds of thoughts,
and for them I don't apologize. If they don't go with the
package, the rest of it's not worth much. Just the same, I
want you to promise me something. When I take you home
tonight, I'll really give you an earful, begging to be asked

[163

up. I want you to tell me no. I want our marriage to be strictly on the beam—the way it is in the books, absolutely according to Hoyle. Do you hear what I say, Grace?"

"I hear you. I'm touched."

"This is Friday night. We can't be married tomorrow, as everything's closed up, license bureau and all. We can't be married Monday. Tuesday we can be. Is that O.K. with you?"

"Then, Tuesday it's a date."

"I'm happy about it. I hope you are."

"Beautifully happy, Clay."

When they got out at Rosemary Park and stood hand in hand once more, listening to the crickets, he whispered: "Maybe they're happy too."

"It's a sweet sound, isn't it?"

"Grace, I want to be asked up."

" . . . But what about our beam? And Hoyle?"

"Do you know what Hoyle *says?*"

"I don't even know who he is—never did know."

"He wrote a book on cards, which tells you a royal straight flush of hearts is the rarest hand there is, happening once in a hundred thousand deals, but sweeping the deck when it comes. Grace, suppose one is waiting for us. Up in your little apartment. Suppose it's the hundred thousandth deal? Do we want to miss it? Do we *dare* to miss it?"

" . . . Clay."

"Yes, Grace?"

"You—come on up."

They were married by the "judge" in the Channel City courthouse, with two clerks as their witnesses, but not on Tuesday, and not with Atlantic City as the place of their honeymoon. Because when at last they could whisper, that same purple night, the subject of it was Sally and what should be done about her. Grace was for calling her up at Mrs.

Granlund's place at Cape May, and calling her up that night, to give her the news, "and then we go on from there." But he put his foot down hard. "She's a special case," he said sternly, "involving me as well as you, and as such rates special treatment. There's no point in jumping the gun. I would say that once this summer is over and we're all back in town, it'll be time enough to call—in a quiet, friendly way, so one thing leads to another. And what I expect is that you and she will go on, pretty much as you always have, with me out on the edges—there, but not often seen, and certainly not heard. That way there'll be no friction. And don't forget: there's not too much to be settled, one way or the other. After all, we'll be in Mankato and won't be seeing much of her."

"There's one thing you've overlooked."

"Yes, Grace? And what's that?"

"*She* must make the announcement. And she can't very well announce something she hasn't been told about."

"Make *what* announcement?"

"Of my marriage—as my nearest kin."

"Well, she's not announcing *my* marriage, I can tell you that right now. In the first place I won't have it, and in the second place she won't. It should come to her, Grace, as a *fait accompli*—not something she has a vote about, from any angle at all."

"Well, of course, nobody votes but us."

"Then she's out. We don't call her."

" . . . I just hate one of those crummy things where two people 'announce their marriage.' It's done—it sometimes has to be done—but I don't like it."

"You want my mother to do it?"

"No, I want *her* to do it—Sally."

"Well, I don't."

So, a bit tearfully, Grace yielded, telling him: "All right, all right—go to sleep. You don't deserve it, but you're spending the night." In the morning she lent him the razor she used on her legs, produced a brand-new toothbrush, all sealed up in its case, and stood smiling through the glass as he took his shower. Then she opened the door and stepped into it too. He laughed, sponging her off, and saying: "To hell with Atlantic City—the beauty contest is here, and so is the winner, Miss America, Mrs. America, Miss World, and Miss Universe, all rolled into one!" Gaily, when they had toweled off, he called the hotel on her phone and canceled the reservation. But when he offered to pay, he was told: "No need, Mr. Lockwood—we'll have that suite rented five minutes from now, maybe sooner. But thanks for your call and thanks for your attitude, which is really most unusual." That out of the way, he said: "O.K., now for Pat."

Pat was delighted, wanting to know all details, and Clay told him: "Matter of fact, she's the artist I told you about. She's finished my picture now and prettied me up in a way that Grant's will be proud of. But I thought: cheaper to marry her than pay her so——"

"That's what you think," said Pat.

"Anh! *Anh!*" said Grace, who happened to hear. Then, grabbing the phone: "Mr. Grant? I wasn't introduced, but my name is Grace Simone, *Mrs.*—a working widow woman, poor but honest. However, something's come up. For reasons we won't go into, mainly the bridegroom's bullheadedness, my family can't be asked to make the announcement, and I was wondering—"

Pat got the point at once, volunteering to take care of everything, engraving, addressing, and mailing. She said she would send him the "dope," what she wanted said, her mailing list, Clay's mailing list, and so on. Then, handing the phone over: "He wants to speak with you."

"Clay," said Pat when Clay spoke again, "that's a damned distinguished voice. Who is she, for God's sake?"

Briefly, quietly, proudly, Clay sketched out Grace's biography, not overlooking "the big job she holds down at Fisher's, our leading department store." Pat was enormously impressed, saying: "I couldn't be better pleased. And Clay: the honeymoon is on us. Don't forget that swing I've been wanting you to take around the circle, to every branch we've got. You take her with you, and we're off on the right foot. Don't forget: maybe we're nothing but butchers, but butchers or not, we're proud. We like manners, we like breeding. We like women with class."

"Don't worry. She's got it."

They decided, with Atlantic City canceled, to postpone things for a day, from Tuesday until Wednesday, "to give me a chance," as she said, "to wind things up at the store and also get something to wear. And to give you the chance, Mr. Lockwood, to put twin beds in your place—that is, if we're using it, as I assume, when we get back from the trip, for the time that's going to remain before we leave for Mankato."

"That's right—thanks for reminding me."

"Get rid of that bed you have!"

The rasp in her voice startled him, and it was a moment before he realized what she meant. Then: "O.K.," he said, "Tuesday it goes out."

"In the meantime you're staying here."

But his real reason for blocking the call to Sally was his concern for what it could mean, the explosion it might cause. He pictured her, when she heard of the wedding plans, as going into a panic at what he might tell, the revelations he might make, the full confession to Grace, as a suitable prelude to marriage. In that, as he learned, he badly misgauged her, but it was what he feared, and he racked his brains for a way to reach her, and reach her before Grace did, to give her reassurance that no such disclosure would come. But how he had no idea. He dared not call her at Bunny's place in Cape May, as he had no way of knowing if

[167

she would be free to talk. And he dared not send her a wire asking her to call him, as she might misunderstand it and go off on some tear that he couldn't anticipate. But on Labor Day he had thought well to visit the shop, make one last holiday check, and see how things were going now that his back was turned. He arrived in late afternoon and spent some time there, not leaving until dusk to keep his dinner date with Grace. His way led up Kennedy Drive, and almost mechanically, passing Elm Street, he glanced toward Sally's house, catching his breath when he saw a light up on the second floor. Circling the block, he parked near the Harlow Theater, walked down, and rang the bell. Nobody came, and then his ear caught the sound of a child's laughter. He rang again, and from an upstairs window Sally called down: "I'll be down in a minute—I can't come just yet. Please wait."

He waited, and then a downstairs light came on, and the door opened. Sally, in black, stiffened when she saw him, and her eyes turned to stones. "What do you want?" she snarled.

"Sally," he said, trying to sound agreeable, "we have business—fairly important business—that should not be discussed out here on the street."

Uneasily, still coldly hostile, she stood aside for him to enter and he stepped first into the hall, then into the room where she had put on the light. By its location, it was a living room but by its furnishings, it was what she had said it was the first evening she visited him, a "storehouse for junk." Against one wall were three cabinets of pink brocade with gold fringe, against another a row of great baskets that crowded against a sofa and two upholstered chairs. Derisively, as he glanced uncomfortably around, she asked: "What's the matter? Afraid something'll jump out at you?"

"Well, it might at that," he said grimly.

"Not at me, it won't."

"Nice when your conscience is clear."

"I asked what you want!" she snapped, pointedly not asking him to sit. "Get at it, if you don't mind. What is this business we have?"

"First: I'm going to marry your mother."

Her eyes dilated, and she stared for some moments. Then: "Are you being funny?" she whispered.

"No, not at all."

"You don't even know my mother."

"On the contrary, I know her very well." He recounted briefly his relations with Grace, especially how they had met, "through that number you gave her each night—my number, you'll recall. She got curious about it and looked it up, finally coming to see me. She approved of me and spent some time promoting the match. With some success, I may add—until, as you know, it somehow fell apart. All that time I was falling for her, and she was, for me. So when she felt, as she said, that you were as cold on me as I seemed to be on you, she felt free to follow her heart, and so, the wedding is going to take place. Don't try to attend—I won't have you there. It would make her happy, though, if you called her up." He waited, studying her, and when he saw she believed him at last, he went on: "However, that's not what I came about. I just wanted to say I've told her nothing, that I'm going to tell her nothing, of what happened a week ago—of your part in it or mine. So you can rest easy and——"

"I had no part in anything."

"Then—O.K. The case is closed."

"Oh, no. Not quite."

" . . . There's something I don't know?"

"There's that girl that I'm going to get."

"Are you talking about Buster?"

"Who do you think I'm talking about? She tried to put it on me, she told those lies about me—and for that I mean to get her."

"Sally, I think you're out of your mind!"

"Am I? Maybe not. The old man played me tricks and choked to death, so it seems. Alec played me tricks and drowned, so it seems. She played me tricks and she'll burn, as it will seem."

"For something we did?"

" 'We?' Who is we?"

"You and I, Sally, both of us."

"I don't even know what you mean!"

"I mean I wonder if you're all there in the head."

He studied her, trying to make up his mind whether this was just venomous talk or if something substantial lay back of it. He couldn't tell, but tried to sound reasonable as he said: "Sally, can't you see you're rocking the boat? That you're playing with TNT? You have the money! You——"

"Money's not all. Oh, no."

" . . . Sally, if you're figuring this as a way to copper-rivet your innocence, it may not work out that way. It could explode in your face in a way to wreck your whole life."

"That's my lookout."

He stood for some moments, rocking back and forth in front of her, then sniffed. "Sally," he said very solemnly, "if I were you, I'd get treatment for that gland. It not only makes you stink but, as *I* would say, leaves you a bit unbalanced."

"Is there something else?"

"You have it straight? What I said?"

"Well, I'm losing no sleep!"

"Then, fine. Did Bunny come back, too?"

"Well, the season's over, isn't it?"

Grace was badly upset when he told her about his visit, and for a time it seemed that the marriage might break up before it even got started. But when Sally called she felt better. "I wouldn't call her effusive," she remarked on hanging up, "but after all, she's involved in it too—as I mustn't forget. She was agreeable enough, though—so perhaps that was the way to handle it, and I'll say no more about it. . . . Shall we eat at the club again? I'm beginning to feel it's 'our place.' "

"So O.K., *but what can she do, what in the hell can she do? Get on with your life, get on with it!*"

20

Grant's, though headquartered in the northern Middle West, mainly covered the Southeast, with branches in Richmond, Atlanta, Miami Beach, Mobile, New Orleans, and Memphis, and so the newlyweds toured Dixie at a time when Dixie was lovely, with autumn perfuming its days while touching its nights with a crisp chill. Pat's red carpet was 1,200 miles long and rolled ahead of them everywhere, so their wants were anticipated, even to their mail, which was waiting at every stop. In Miami Beach, to their great amusement, they received the announcement of their own marriage and at once called Pat to thank him. "I thought it would give you a bang," he said, evidently proud of himself. "How was that for all due deliberate speed?" Clay said it was "pure magic," and then Grace took the phone, with appreciative comments on "that paper and the engraving— oh, my, how beautifully it was done." Once more, when Clay took the phone again, Pat admired "that well-bred voice," and Clay felt very proud. But at Mobile, Pat called them to acknowledge the picture's arrival, they having called Mr. Gumpertz, their last hectic day in Channel City, and had him take it over for forwarding. Pat, after complimenting Grace, told Clay: "Listen, my grandfather's picture, my father's, and mine all look as though painted by a friend of the mayor's, which of course they were. But this is a beautiful thing—a real work of art, which is something I know about even if I don't know meat. So I hope you're proud of who you're married to."

She revealed much savvy at entertaining, not only its basic principles but also its special angles, at the hotel cocktail parties they gave for Grant's executives and their wives. "The trick," she whispered, in a dark, conspiratorial way, "is in knowing where to splurge and where to pare the cheese. And the main thing, Clay, is champagne—it's the key to the big economies. So it costs, you say? Yes, but look what it saves. You try wetting their whistles with the standard line of mixed drinks, and you have to have a bartender, as well as an endless assortment of liquors he'll tell you he has to have—everything from quinine water to Cinzano. And once opened, that booze is all down the drain. We dare not take it with us, as we don't know the laws in these states, and even one bottle of Angostura could get your car confiscated. On top of which, you'll need an extra room where he can set up his bar. But with champagne you don't need him: the waiter we have can open, pour, and pass. You offer champagne at the start, and who turns it down? Everyone loves it, and if there is one nut who wants Scotch, O.K., you give it to him with your own lily-white hands. You have it stashed with a bowl of rocks under the buffet table—and that takes care of him. For the rest, the champagne is opened as we need it, and extra bottles go back—it's the standard procedure. So, if that's understood, we'll get to the fine points, like the kind of canapés we have."

But, though all this no doubt reflected her years abroad, in one respect, as she herself admitted, she was a "one-hundred-percent American hick": she always, on Sunday morning, sent the boy out for the hometown paper and then stretched herself out "to see what's going on—especially what Fisher's is featuring." In New Orleans, with brunch out of the way,

174]

she was comfortably flat on her stomach in their sitting room, with *The Pilot* strewn all around her, when she gave a sharp exclamation: "*Well!*" And then: "It's about time, it certainly is!"

She was in mules and crimson kimono, he in slippers and monogrammed robe, with a program about to be played in Washington tuned in on TV. "Yeah?" he inquired languidly. "What's about time, Grace?"

"They've arrested that girl, the one that killed poor Alec. That assistant he had in the act. That Buster."

" . . . Grace, are you sure she killed Alexis?"

"Well, they know what they're doing, I think."

"They've been known to make mistakes."

"On 'Perry Mason,' that's all."

"Grace, what would she kill him for?"

"The insurance, for one thing."

"She'd risk her own neck for that?"

"What neck? She jumped clear, didn't she? By a funny coincidence, after refusing to fasten her seat belt, as he begged her to."

"Can I see the paper, please?"

Staring at Page 1, he felt himself go slack at the picture he saw, of Buster in ecdysiast attire, and at another picture too, a smaller inset of a woman in uniform cap. This, he learned, was Policewoman Elizabeth Galbraith, who had "broken the case" by getting the parking attendant to talk, the boy who had stood around while the quarrel went on between Buster and Mr. Alexis and who had heard her "make threats." Until now, it appeared, the boy had refused to talk or admit he had heard anything, maintaining he had been "busy getting the car out." There was quite a lot more, especially about Miss Galbraith and what she had done, and the boy, whose name was Norman (Bud) Jones. It appeared he had been held as a material witness in $2,000 bail, "which was furnished by a bondsman."

Clay lay on the bed, one of the twin beds, in the bedroom, massaging his flaccid face, not quite sure how he got there. Then he put in a call to Nat Pender, getting a flash of the jitters at having to find his pen and take down the Pender home number, when Channel City Information looked it up for him. Then he put in the person-to-person, and when at last Mr. Pender came on, talking with a reasonable imitation of easy affability, "Nat," he said, "Clay Lockwood—say, I owe you a million pardons for bothering you at home and on Sunday this way, but I more or less felt I had to."

"You calling about Buster?" Mr. Pender interrupted.

"That's right. I just saw the paper."

"Clay, that girl's in trouble, a lot worse than the paper says. Because what's back of it isn't Liz Galbraith, though count on her, of course, to get her mug printed any chance she gets. Actually it's the wife who got to Bud Jones, and in a way to make him dangerous. I mean, after she got through there's no way to call him off, make him get cold feet, or listen to reason."

"You mean Mrs. Alexis."

"Yeah—she'd be better off with a tiger."

Quickly Mr. Pender sketched the background on the case. Bud, he said, had been soft on Buster himself, but for some reason hadn't minded her relationship with Mr. Alexis. So he had loyally "clammed," as Mr. Pender put it, about the quarrel on the lot, realizing it could mean trouble. But then "Mrs. Alexis got in it, having long talks with him out on the parking lot at night, and in the daytime asking him down to visit her at the hotel. She's put the house on sale, given up her Portico job, and moved into the Chinquapin-Plaza, with a maid and children's nurse, and the boy was flattered when she invited him for long, intimate talks. Did you know he talks with a stammer? Little by little she began telling him of Buster's imitations of how he talks. Clay, I doubt if Buster did it—it doesn't sound like her, she's a good-hearted girl, though dumb. And it's Mrs. Alexis, it seems, that has a gift at such imitations—she's been in show business herself. *Anyway*, she did a snow job for real, and that jerk hates Buster now. That's why he can't be seen, by her or anyone. When she ripened it up and rang Liz Galbraith about it, the rest was a foregone conclusion."

Clay listened with rising dismay and then broke in: "O.K., Nat, and thanks for filling me in—but what I called about: are you still on the case?"

"Oh, she's retained me, yes."

"How do you mean, retained you?"

Mr. Pender spoke at some length in highly ethical terms, but when Clay pressed him, explained that Buster's insurance, "which was paid her some weeks ago," made it possible for him to invoke the twenty-five to fifty percent rule, "twenty-five percent of recoveries, as retainer for taking the case, fifty percent if we go to court. Or in other words, it seems fair enough that she pay me six and a quarter thousand down, with another six and a quarter due when she's tried—which it looks as though she's going to be." Clay was staggered, but knew he must pick up the tab. He said: "Nat, I feel I should pay that fee—I have reasons we needn't go into. So when she sends her check, will you hold it? Pending receipt of *my* check? I'll mail it here now today." And then, doing some mental arithmetic: "Or wait a minute, Nat. I don't keep that kind of money lying around, and it'll pinch me in on my trip if I send the whole six and a quarter grand. So can I send you half? Part now, the rest to come when I get back and can sell off some stuff that I have? As I say, I have reasons—"

"Clay," said Mr. Pender, "whatever you say is fine, and I don't ask your reasons. She's a damned sweet kid, that anyone's entitled to go for and—" Clay opened his mouth to protest it was "nothing like that," but then realized it might be better if Mr. Pender thought it was "that" instead of something else. He let it ride, and when Mr. Pender asked where he was, told him. "But of course!" exclaimed Mr. Pender. "How stupid of me not to remember! You're on your honeymoon—and congratulations. My wife knows the bride and can't say enough in her praise!"

"Thanks," said Clay. "And thank your wife."

"O.K., it's going to cost, but you couldn't do any less, and at least with this guy she can't lose. Now! Quit your glawming, get on with your life!"

He did not, however, at once go back to the sitting room. He went to the bathroom and shaved, then got into the tub. The water was running when the tap came on the door, and he hadn't heard the phone. "Mr. Nat Pender calling," said Grace, through the door. "Will you take it? Or shall I have him call later?" He took it and listened while Nat revised their arrangement. "Clay," he said, "we kept talking about various things, and I didn't get quite caught up until we said good-by. Forget that check for part—forget *any* check, boy. I wouldn't louse your trip, not for anything. When you get back will be time—and she gets her check back tomorrow. Now forget her, forget me, forget everything but your wife and having a real nice time."

He dressed and at last went back to the sitting room. The TV was still on, but Grace had got herself dressed, in white faille, and the paper was neatly folded on top of the radiator. His eyes as he met hers were blank, with the look card players have, and also criminals facing the law. He glanced out at the bright sunlight, said: "Hm—looks like a nice day after all. They have nothing but rain in this place, but when the sun does shine it's pretty." Then he sat down and watched the Baltimore Colts run over the Washington Red-skins, or "Skins," as the announcer called them.

"May we have that off?" she asked in a moment.

"Why, sure, if it bores you."

He snapped the TV off. "Mr. Nat Pender," she said, walking over to face him, "is a criminal lawyer. What business does he have with you?"

"*Hey!* Who wants to know?"

"I do. Your wife. Remember?"

"Why—he called on a certain matter."

"Clay, I asked you, what matter?"

"Well—actually it was a call-back, about something he forgot to tell me. I had called *him,* as a matter of fact."

"About that girl?"

"Could have been. Well—yes."

"He was her lawyer before—he held a press conference for her before we left Channel City. Clay, you had something to do with that?"

"Well, I don't just now recollect, I——"

"*Answer me!*"

He hadn't been meeting her eye, but now, when he had to, saw a woman of ice, once a corporation executive herself, who couldn't be fobbed off with vague evasions. "O.K.," he said, "I may have."

"Did you pay his bill?"

On that he grew disagreeable, saying, "What's it to you?" and other ugly things. Her face, as she stared down at him, didn't change. "In other words," she persisted, "you paid him?"

"Well, goddamit, suppose I did?"

"Why?"

"I've told you! I don't think she's guilty!"

"That's her lookout, isn't it? Is it up to you to pay the attorney of every girl who's falsely accused? Why did you pay this man?"

"Listen, there's nothing between her and me!"

"I didn't say there was."

"Then why the third degree? Why——"

"You did it, that's why."

"I already said I did! How many times do I——"

"*Stop it!* Stop pretending I mean one thing when I'm talking about something else. There's only one explanation for this, one explanation that explains. You drove that car she saw, the one she thought was Sally's. You killed Alec. Didn't you?"

She stood like something Greek, like something carved in marble, while he slumped in his chair, his eyes not focusing, his mouth slobbery. Then: "Yes," he whispered.

She went to the window and stood for a while, looking out at the river, where it wound around the town. When she spoke, her voice was still cold. "What was the quarrel about?" she asked. "Why did Sally break with you?"

Falteringly at first, by jerks and gasps and gulps, with growing coherence, as confession seemed to steady him, he recounted his scenes with Sally, her visit to him and his to her at her house, and then plunged on to the visit from Buster and his talks with Mr. Pender on the phone. "That's all!" he broke out presently. "It's all I know to tell you! If you have any questions to ask, get it over with now, *please!* I'm not enjoying this any! And I'm not one damned bit sure that I'll be able to take it if you start up again—*later on.*"

"You intend to stand by this girl?"

"I can't do less! I can't walk off and leave her! If you think I can, if you think I'm going to, you're nuts."

"I'm not nuts."

So far, though their voices hadn't been loud, they had been bellowing over a chasm, so far as close communication was concerned. Now, however, she went over, lifted the white faille dress, knelt beside him, and took his head in her

180]

arms. "I had to know where we stand," she whispered, "or I couldn't make any sense. Now, Clay, *I* speak. I tell you: *"I'm* standing by *you!* . . . If you want me to!"

"You needn't. You don't have to stand by a rat."

"I see no rats in here."

"Look around. Maybe there is one."

"All I see is a wonderful guy that I love, that I'm married to, that's my husband. That comes first, before anyone else—daughter, grandchild, anyone. I love them, I can't pretend that I don't. But you come first, and I stand by if you want me. . . . If you don't, say it, and I'll get on the plane and go home."

"Are you being funny, Grace?"

"Then, you do want me?"

"More than anything on this earth."

"Then, *that's* settled."

She pulled away, sitting on her heels, as though to go on, but he interrupted: "Do we *have* to keep talking about it? If you're with me, if you can find it in your heart not to despise me too much—then that's enough, for now. I'm kind of—!"

"Groggy?"

"Sick, Grace. Sick *of* it!"

"Darling, there's more to say, that will——"

"Then say it, get it said!"

"That will make you feel better, I *think!*"

She climbed in his lap, covered his face with tender little kisses, went on: "It might help a little bit, perhaps, if I stood on the edge and said kind things to you down there in the pit. It's not enough! I owe you more, not from duty, but because there *is* more! *I'm down in the pit with you!*"

"Hey! I'm in a pit, all right. But you—?"

"Darling! If I had listened to you that very first night, and not only to you but my heart, none of this would have happened! You made passes at me, beautiful, insolent passes, that made my heart go bump. I could have yielded to you

[181

and taken you from her right then! You wanted to be taken, because of what she intended, of what you knew she intended, of what *I* knew she intended! I burrowed my head in the sand, but I knew the truth in my heart. And so I made myself say no, made myself go on, with my slick, smart-aleck intrigue, using you as a cat's-paw, as I thought. So you can move over, if you think it's your private pit! I'm in it with you!"

She pushed, wriggled, and forced herself into his chair, her dress slipping up, her legs twined over his, her mouth on his.

21

Channel City looked just the same when they got back, in mid-November, as it had when they had gone away except that the leaves had turned brown, yellow, and red. For the effect on his morale, she had insisted that Mr. Pender be paid the full $6,250 he asked and that she be permitted, as a lift on the money problem, to send her personal check, for deposit in his account, for $5,000. She also made him complete the trip, and they went to Memphis, St. Louis, and Denver, winding up at Mankato. Here they stayed with Pat at his estate on the Minnesota River, and he really did his stuff, bringing things to a climax with a big white-tie reception, followed by a dance, at the Ben-Pay Hotel. She was lovely in formal crimson, the labella of her orchids exactly matching her gown. She was vain of her affinity with these flowers, proclaiming that "they like you or they don't—and as mine last ten days, it just goes to show." Pat, impressed by such things, became her devoted pal, beauing her around, inspecting the picture with her, and inviting her to the unveiling—"which of course can't come just yet." When at last they got home and went to his apartment, he was almost himself again, giving a fine imitation of a brisk, masterful executive when he called on Mr. Pender to find out how things stood.

It seemed they stood very badly, "and for no good reason,

Clay." The case against Buster, he said, "is wholly circum-stantial, and circumstantial cases are weak. I might even have got it quashed except for one thing. This girl won't *let* me attack the case against her, this web of circumstance that's been put together mainly at the wife's instigation. She insists on a case of her own—that the wife did it, that she killed her husband, by driving up without lights, banging a horn in his ear, and causing him to swerve. She insists that she saw the car, that she got its number, and nothing that I can say, no amount of dope the police collected about it, can unlock her from that story. I've explained to her that to set up such a defense she'll have to take the stand—she can't stand on her rights and say nothing. In effect she'll have to start another case and prosecute it herself. She says she won't have a defense 'that says I'm guilty, only you can't prove it.' That, of course, is something I can't disregard—it has that strange, sweet smell of the truth. But, allowing for that, it's all wrong! It forgets something I can't quite say to her—not in so many words. Clay, you may be fond of this girl—I can't know how you feel—but her *life's* at stake and I'd better say what I mean. She's what she is: a chantoosie, a striptoosie, a——"

"Flip-floosie? Is that what you're getting at?"

"Well, you said it, Clay. I didn't."

"O.K. She's that—and looks it, Nat."

"And talks it—she sounds like one of those twerps that Jack Benny digs up to do a bit on his show. . . . I'm sorry, Clay, if I——"

"It's O.K. Her life's at stake, after all!"

Mr. Pender was still obviously under the impression that Clay's interest in Buster was personal, and Clay wanted to set him right. He realized, however, that correction of one impression might very well lead to another, and so once more he let the misapprehension ride. Mr. Pender went on: "Well, since you don't mind discussing it freely, I can tell you that once she starts this line, John Kuhn will rip her apart. He's not a wolf at his job—just a good lawyer that's state's attorney. *But,* he's a damned good lawyer who takes his job very serious. And where she'll lead with her chin is from having this idea that the wife was just a bitch who came between two loving hearts and started causing them trouble, winding up with this murder. It may have been that—I can't say it wasn't. But as John Kuhn is going to develop it, *she* was the one who broke up Alexis' marriage, and also she had boy-friends on the side. Clay, you weren't the only one—you might just as well know it. Daytime, she ran a free-wheeling joint. And—well, you see what I'm up against?"

"When do you go to trial?"

"Monday."

"Then—I'll send you your check———"

"Clay, I told you, forget the check! Whenever———"

"You'll get it—before you go to court."

"Clay, there's one more thing."

"Yeah? Which is?"

"Something's going to be made of Buster's nagging Alexis to climb up on a ladder to check an installation of overhead rails. But she says it was your idea."

"That's right, I told him to do it."

Briefly he recounted the conversation in the cold room, including the Mexico City anecdote, and wound up: "I urged on him the importance of getting them level—any rails that might be put in."

"Would you take the stand and say that?"

After hesitating, Clay said: "All right, Nat."

"I know it's asking a lot," said Mr. Pender, "to speak for this tramp in public—but it'll help her in more ways than one. For one thing, it'll ventilate this charge that she spent the whole summer scheming to break his neck. For another, to have someone of substance up there, to say something on her behalf, will help most of all. In a criminal case it's not only what's said. Who says it is still more important. And Mike Dominick won't be much help."

"Oh, Mike's O.K.—except for the blue chin."

"Right! Except for that, he's fine."

Monday, though nearly a week off, seemed to fly in: too many things had to be done. Clay hated it, getting U.S. bonds from his box, taking them to his broker, and having them sold for cash, but Grace eased things by offering to go along. At the Channel City National Bank, as well as at Stone, Stone & Johns, she chatted with the clerks, managing to small the thing down and make it seem quite casual. When they left the bank, she handed him a deposit slip for $2,000, this representing another withdrawal from her personal checking account, almost all she had—she having managed to visit the teller without his seeing her do it. He was ashamed, and yet at the same time proud, that she would do such a thing with such offhand ease. At last, when they got home that day, he screwed up his courage to tell her of what he had promised Nat Pender, to take the stand for Buster. But instead of being upset she actually seemed glad. "The one thing that bothered me," she confessed, "was that we were trying to buy you out—buy ourselves out, as I'm in it as well as you. It sounds good, that we'd put up twelve and a half thousand bucks to help this girl in distress. But we *have* twelve and a half thousand bucks, or did have, and after all it's nothing but money. This, though, goes beyond that. It proves that we'll do what has to be done. Now! Perhaps that makes you feel better!"

There were other things too, but what frazzled his nerves most were the endless telephone calls, from friends, her friends and his friends, from people they hardly knew, from people they didn't know at all—requesting the pleasure of their company at lunch, at cocktails, at dinner. At first she sidestepped these invitations, with innocuous little fibs: "Oh, how sweet of you to remember us—and of course we'd be delighted—except for the hectic time we're having, and will have for a week or two—all sorts of things have come up— we're here today and gone tomorrow—we're like bats, flitting hither, thither, and yon—but *could* you give us a raincheck? So when things do settle down, and we have some time for our friends, before we leave for the West—?" But things grew more and more complicated, her voice shriller and shriller, his mood worse and worse from the jitters. And so at last, after one particularly bad time on the phone, she marched herself back to the bedroom, remaining a while. When she reappeared she was hatted, coated, and gloved and had a packed bag in her hand. "Come on," she said grimly. "We're going to Rosemary Park." She still had her apartment, not having had time so far to store her things and sublet it. He took her in his arms and kissed her, and they moved to her little modernist place. There, for their few days remaining, they had peace. The phone did ring occasionally, but they grinned at each other and let it.

At last Monday came, and for a long time Clay stared incredulously around the courtroom in Channel City's austere courthouse. It was crowded, but with the help of a bailiff, one of Nat Pender's friends, Clay found a seat on a bench near the rail without any trouble. And what he found so hard to believe was that a place so warmly pleasant, its ceiling so aglow from soft indirect lighting, its acoustics so quiet that footfalls made no sound, could hold life or death in the balance, for anyone at all, especially someone as harmless as Buster. Even the two flags, the red, white, and blue of the United States to the right of the bench, the gold and black of Maryland to its left, were of such beautiful silk that they hardly implied this power, or anything, except poetic patriotism. Suddenly, as he pondered this paradox, Buster came in by a side door, escorted by a policewoman and met by Mr. Pender, who appeared from somewhere and brought her to a table inside the rail. She still had on her black dress, with a small black shell hat, and a beige coat on her arm. She was thinner than Clay remembered her, paler, and infinitely more dignified. She saw him, smiled, and gave him a little wave. He nodded and tried to smile back. Then he felt eyes upon him and turned to find Sally there, at the other end of the bench he was sitting on. At that moment a man appeared at her side, shaking hands, whom Clay identified, from his pictures in the paper, as John Kuhn, the prosecutor. He appeared to be in his forties, a medium-sized man, dark, with some distinction about him, a point Clay noted with relief. He had dreaded a bully, knowing only too well his own reaction to such men, which was to turn bully himself. Mr. Kuhn had scarcely gone through the rail and taken his place at a table across from Mr. Pender's than a bailiff appeared by the Maryland flag, banged three times with a gavel, and announced: "This honorable court is now in session," while simultaneously everybody stood up and a judge appeared from below, taking his seat on the bench. His name, Clay had learned, was Warfield, he being of the same family as one of the state's governors. He was perhaps in his sixties, with pink face, silver hair, and mild, humane expression. In his robes, he had his share of the good looks his family was noted for.

"State of Maryland versus Edith Conlon."

Told to rise, Buster did so, and was informed of the charge against her: First-degree murder, in that she "did willfully and with malice aforethought, compass, contrive, and cause the death of one Alexander Gorsuch."

Asked "How do you plead?" she let go with a hot, defiant blast, snarling: "Not guilty, *that's how I plead!*"

Her tone got a gasp of surprise from the crowd, of anger from the bailiff, who used his gavel again. "You stop banging that thing at me!" snapped Buster, advancing on him. "You asked how I plead and I told you! 'Not guilty!' as I'm entitled to say and expect to keep on saying!"

"The defendant will take her seat."

Judge Warfield was quite stern, and Mr. Pender, after leading Buster to her chair, said ingratiatingly: "May it please the court?" and then asked that allowance be made "for the state of my client's emotions: a six-week stay in jail plus the accusation she faces don't exactly produce a tranquil spirit."

"This court," said Judge Warfield, "is not insensible to such considerations, but I intend to have decorum. Miss Conlon, do you hear? You will show respect for this court."

"I have respect for this court," said Buster, rising again. "But I'd like some respect too, and he can stop banging at me."

"The court has respect for you."

The ghost of a smile played on Judge Warfield's handsome face, and as Buster sat down again he proceeded to the selection of a jury. Clay listened as the talesmen were examined, trying to make himself follow, but being distracted from within by the surge of pride that he felt in this cheap, baffling girl and the courage she had shown, standing up for her rights, or what she felt were her rights. The thing went on, and by lunchtime only five jurors were chosen, four men and a woman. "You'll notice," said Mr. Pender, over a tray in the courthouse cafeteria, "I'm leaning heavy on men—more broad-minded, Clay. Her danger is that she'll be convicted not of committing murder but of being—what was that word you used?—a flip-floosie. I got to remember that, it covers a lot of ground. Well, men aren't bothered by it so much. But men-only are bad too. Couple of girls in there, of a nice,

sensible kind, will head off the smoking-car jokes while the
ballots are being taken. So, as of now, we're doing all right."

The thing went on all afternoon, and it was after five
when the twelve were accepted, ten men and two women,
and Judge Warfield recessed until next morning. Home with
Grace, Clay told everything: his eye clash with Sally, Buster's outbreak, the judge's amusement, Mr. Pender's ap-
proach to the jury, and the kind of panel they had. "O.K., I
thought—they look like decent people that can take a reasonable view." She listened, preoccupied with dinner: a
fragrant martini, which she made by a formula of her own,
terrapin soup, duck, baked potato, peas, salad, and ice
cream. With the duck she gave him Chambertin, in all ways
coddling his inner man and making him feel loved. After
washing up, she put him to bed early, then climbed in with
him and cuddled his head on her breast. He inhaled her with
deep content, saying: "Well, make a long story short: the
main thing today, from my end, was that guy John Kuhn. I
have no doubt he's tough—all prosecutors are and no use
squawking on that. But toughness I don't mind—after ten
years selling meat, what does it mean to me? Not a thing—
I'm used to it. It's all in a day's work. But at least he's a
gentleman! What I was dreading, Grace, was one of these
louts. But this guy, to every one of those people, had manners. Even the roughnecks, the ones in the blue flannel
shirts, he called 'Mr.,' and always remembered their names.
Same with the women: it was 'Miss' or 'Mrs.,' and invariably
with respect. If he acts that way with me, it's all that I ask.
Maybe you think I'm cockeyed but——"

"I don't at all. I know how you feel. I glory in you for it—I
wouldn't have you different. *Now*, if you're all talked out,
hold onto your hat. Who do you think called?"

"I bite. Who?"

"Sally. Around lunchtime."

"Yeah? And what did she want?"

"As she *said*, to ask how I was and how I'd enjoyed my trip. As I *think*, to find out what I've been told."

"And what did you say, Grace?"

"Nothing. That Mankato was simply swell."

"Just—chitter-chatter?"

"That's it."

"Did she buy it, do you think?"

"With her you never know. But—she *could* have."

She subsided, and he held her close for a time, but then she started again. "Clay," she whispered, "I had to ask too. I couldn't do less, of course."

"You mean, how she's been getting along."

"Yes—and how someone *else* has."

"Oh? The little boy?"

"Yes, of course."

"Well? And how *has* he been getting along?"

"The way she tells it is *famously.*" Clay started as she reproduced Sally's voice, but she went on, "He just loves everything: the suite she has on the twentieth floor of the Chinquapin-Plaza; the new nurse she got for him, an English girl named Lizette; his kindergarten school; his pony out at the stables; his teddy bear; his sleep suit—and of course his little friends, Bunny's kids. Clay, all the time she was talking something went through my mind. After we've moved, when we're equipped to take care of a child . . ."

"You'd like to ask him out? Is that it?"

"I'd give *anything* if we could!"

"We'll—take it under advisement."

"Clay, he's such a dear, sweet little boy! And until you came along he was my life. He was——"

"I thought we were going to have some of our own."

"You bet we are! Oh, I haven't forgotten *them!*"

"O.K.—then as soon as this is over . . ."

"We'll start working on them!"

She kissed him and then whispered for twenty minutes, with all an artist's exactitude, about pregnant women, "their big bellies, the haunted look in their eyes, their craving for lollipops, for canned peaches, for everything under the sun. God's caricatures, aren't they? Clay, a woman big with child is the most beautiful thing in the world—and that's what I want to be: big with child again, *your* child."

"That'll be swell, won't it, having a child in the house that you can't look in the eye because you killed his father. That's one grand scheme that you can kid her out of."

22

Mr. Kuhn was brief in his opening statement, a bit regretful, and devastatingly to the point. The state, he said, would prove that the defendant "killed the deceased while riding beside him, by the simple trick of jerking the wheel of his car, jumping clear when it swerved, and leaving him to plunge, by a momentum he couldn't arrest, over a bank that collapsed under him, into eight feet of water." Her motives, he went on, were crude, "but wholly comprehensible, if also wholly wicked." First, she wanted revenge "on a man who had been her lover, but who on the death of his father had reconsidered his mode of life, and decided to patch up his marriage if he could. This man had a wife, as the defendant knew he had from her first meeting with him, as the wife introduced her to him." Second she wanted cash, "twenty-five thousand dollars in insurance she stood to collect, provided his death took place before the policy lapsed—and it still had two months to run." Then piece by piece he fitted his case together, stressing that "this was no caprice, no sudden fit of temper," and citing an episode in the nightclub, "where the defendant nagged and urged and goaded the deceased to climb a ladder, to observe, as she told him, if overhead rails were level, but actually in the hope he would fall—and break his neck." In a shocked, low voice, Mr. Kuhn added: "He did fall—he did not break his neck." And then, he went on, "she took her last desperate step—intruded herself into his car and flung him down to his death." He admitted that nobody saw this, that "our case is circumstantial." Nevertheless, he said, "there was a witness, silent, but eloquent, in the shape of a seat belt, which was fastened, but jammed back of the seat." But his best witness, he concluded, would be the defendant herself, who had scarcely reached the hospital "before she began making statements, copious statements, to the police—every one of which turned out false."

He elected to start with "background," and his first witness was Sally. A thready tremor of fear wriggled through Clay's heart as the bailiff called: "Mrs. Sally Gorsuch," and wriggled again as she whirled in front of him, where he sat in the same seat he had had the day before. She was in a black wool suit and soft black felt hat, and made a pale, ladylike picture as she climbed to the witness box, held up her hand to swear, and gave her name in a quiet voice, so quiet that Judge Warfield admonished her, "Louder, Mrs. Gorsuch—speak so the jury can hear." Under Mr. Kuhn's skillful questioning, she told the story of her marriage, how as a high-school student she had met a young magician, gone to work in his act, and married him. "Then, very soon," she went on, "I was expecting my child and couldn't work any more. He needed someone, and I remembered a girl who'd been in looking for work, who had a pretty figure, and was about the right size—a magician's assistant has to be small, so she can climb into baskets, slip out of cabinets, and so on, without having to squeeze. Her name was Edith Conlon—she's sitting right over there. I sent for her and introduced her to him."

After that Sally's manner changed. With eyes on the floor, face pinking up, she went on: "Then in just a few days I began to suspect my husband, and rumors began reaching me. I accused him then and made him admit the truth, that he was unfaithful to me, with Edith. I locked my door from then on, and we were married in name only. Then, after some time, at least two years, I would say, my husband's father died, and his attitude seemed to change. He began hinting that we should 'make up,' as he called it. To that I said nothing, and don't know now how I felt. I had been horribly hurt, and whether I could forget, even though I forgave, I have no idea at all. But I thought I should listen to him and to give him the chance to talk. To get things started somehow, I told him one day that as I would be up that night much later than usual, entertaining my mother at dinner, with two friends I had also invited, we could talk after they left—if he could come home early. I meant, as he well understood, if he omitted his visit to Edith. And he said: 'It's a date.' It was the last time I saw him alive. He didn't come at all, and I supposed he had changed his mind. But next day came the horrible news that he was dead. And next night, Mr. Kuhn, came the still more horrible news that Edith had seen my car, or had told the police that she had, driving away from the accident. And the day after *that* I found, tucked away in my husband's desk, a bill for insurance premiums on a policy I knew nothing about!"

Sally's voice became strident, and her eyes took on a glitter not quite so ladylike. During her recital, as the words "suspect," "rumor," "admit," and "suppose" kept getting into it, the judge looked toward Mr. Pender, as Clay did, apparently assuming he would object. However, he didn't. He said nothing until it was his turn to cross-examine, and then, after studying his notes as though baffled, he asked: "Mrs. Gorsuch, when you found this bill for insurance premiums, what did you do about it?"

"I—had it looked into at once."

"By whom, if you don't mind?"

" . . . By—the police, of course."

"Why the police?"

"Well, why not? They were in charge, weren't they?"

"Object!" exclaimed Mr. Kuhn, as though bored. "What she did is evidence. Why she did it is immaterial, incompetent, and irrelevant, as counsel well knows."

"Withdraw the question," said Mr. Pender.

Once more consulting his notes, and once more seemingly puzzled, he asked: "Did you, Mrs. Gorsuch, before calling the police, call the insurance company?"

"No—I had no reason to."

"No reason? On finding a premium bill for insurance payable, now that your husband was dead? And possibly payable to you?"

"It was payable to her, Mr. Pender. To Edith."

"Did it so state on the bill?"

" . . . I—don't just now recollect."

"What difference does it make?" asked Mr. Kuhn. "We have the bill. Here it is—take it, Nat. Enter it as an exhibit— let her see it—and let's get on!"

"I can try my own case, thanks."

"I'm not much impressed," said the judge, "by sparring matches between counsels. If it matters, Mr. Pender, why can't the bill be entered?"

"What matters," said Mr. Pender, "is this witness—her animus against the defendant, her part in this prosecution, and above all, her veracity."

"You mean, if she knew the beneficiary—?"

"She knew about the insurance."

"You may answer," the judge told Sally.

"Did the bill name Miss Conlon?" asked Mr. Pender.

"I said I don't recollect!"

Sally almost screamed it, her eyes flashing at Mr. Pender, so several jurors leaned forward in surprise, seeing a woman very different from the quiet widow in black who had first taken the stand. And even the judge frowned. "Mrs. Gorsuch," he said quietly, "this passes credence. You're not on trial here—you can't decide which questions you answer and which you don't. You're a witness for the state, and you're under oath. You must answer or be found in contempt."

"All right, then, it didn't."

"Then you already knew who the beneficiary was?"

"All right, suppose I did?"

"And you *did* know about the insurance—it was not something you knew nothing about, as you so affectingly told us just a few moments ago?"

"What difference does *that* make?"

Mr. Kuhn barked it, but Mr. Pender answered mildly: "None—except to make her admit—let the jury hear her admit—that in one respect at least she has not been telling the truth."

"Answer," said the judge.

"All right, but it slipped my mind!" Sally snapped it peevishly, but two of the jurors laughed.

"And so you called the police?"

"I certainly did."

"With the first evidence against Miss Conlon?"

"But not the last, Mr. Pender. And so you get it straight, anything I could do to help convict her, that woman sitting there, who tried to put this on me, I did do, and mean to keep on doing."

Hand-clapping broke out in the rear of the court, and the bailiff banged his gavel. But the jurors stared at Sally, struck once more, perhaps, by her vitriolic manner. "Thank you," said Mr. Pender.

"Is that all?" asked Sally.

"No, Mrs. Gorsuch. Not quite."

Mr. Pender now began probing the marriage and why it had broken up. Once more Mr. Kuhn objected, and as the judge turned to him Mr. Pender reflected a moment and then began to talk. "Your honor," he said, "the defense hasn't opened its case, and so I haven't outlined what it's going to be. But in the light of these objections, it might be well if I cleared things up a bit. Left to my own devices, I would have preferred a simple defense, the immemorial stratagem of shooting this case full of holes, having Miss Conlon say nothing, and let the jury's good sense give this preposterous accusation the rebuke it so richly deserves. However, I'm stopped: my client won't have this defense. She won't come to court and let me, as she feels, tacitly admit her guilt 'except that they can't prove it.' She insists on the defense she has made from the beginning, that she saw Mrs. Gorsuch's car at the scene of the death, that this car, by sneaking up without lights and suddenly blowing its horn, caused the deceased to swerve, and thereby killed him. That's what she told the police, and that's what, says the state, 'turned out to be false.' And I thought it was, I confess. I tried to persuade her of the part imagination might have played in what she saw that night, and I tried in vain. And then, *and then*"—here Mr. Pender let emotion creep into his voice—"it devolved on me, became my duty to her, to look around a bit, to ascertain if evidence existed that her story *could* be true. Not only, I emphasize, that she *thinks* she's speaking the truth. That I've never doubted. But also that the truth *could* be as she speaks it!"

"*Anything* can be," said Judge Warfield sharply.

"Except, says the state, Mrs. Gorsuch's guilt."

"She's not on trial, I remind you."

"I hope not—I don't want the job of proving her guilt. My job is to prove reasonable doubt of Miss Conlon's guilt, *on the basis of Mrs. Gorsuch's possible guilt!* 'Anything can be,' as your honor so cogently says, but this parcel of guilt has been placed out of reach by the state, up high on a separate shelf, with a *don't-open-until-Christmas* sticker on it. Your honor, I must open it up. I must know what's inside. I must be allowed to find out."

"Suppose nothing's inside?" asked Mr. Kuhn.

198]

"Then Miss Conlon will pay, very dearly."

"If you have a case——?" Mr. Kuhn barely murmured it, but Mr. Pender took him up quickly. "Ah, yes," he cut in. "We know this ancient adage: 'If you have a case, try it—if not, try your accusers.' There's another, still more ancient, one of the oldest our language knows: '*Murder will out!*' The defense doesn't fear this ancient saw—it wants this murder out in the open, where it belongs. Why does the state insist on tying it up?"

"Objection withdrawn," said Mr. Kuhn.

"Proceed," said Judge Warfield.

"Mrs. Gorsuch," said Mr. Pender, "could we go back just a bit to your husband's change of attitude after his father died. Did he say anything to you that explained his reason for this?"

"Well, I don't know. He was upset."

"By—grief, could we say?"

"Why, yes. Of course. Naturally."

"At the millions he now stood to inherit?"

But once more Mr. Kuhn objected. "In the name of God," he asked, "what do the millions have to do with this case?"

"May it please the court," said Mr. Pender, "I'm glad the state has asked. The millions could have been—I don't say they were, but they could have been—the motive this lady had to wish her husband dead." And then solicitously, colloquially, to Mr. Kuhn: "You remember them motives, don't you? Miss Conlon's yen for revenge? On a guy that done her wrong? He done Mrs. Gorsuch wrong, as a faithless husband to her, and we've had one flash already of her vindictive spirit. The money Miss Conlon would make—remember the cash? The twenty-five thousand bucks? Mrs. Gorsuch stood to make millions by her husband's death. Your case, my young friend, has boomeranged."

"I'd say yours is sheer name-blackening."

"Yes," said Judge Warfield. "So far, Mr. Pender, with

nothing to back it up except the claim that it 'could be,' that's about all it amounts to. Once again, *anything* can be."

"Your honor, I *have* positive evidence."

"I must have some clue to its nature before I let you proceed with this line of questioning. So far, it's only a smear."

"Its nature, your honor, is simple. The state makes quite a point about the police, how they proved the statements false that Miss Conlon made to them. I'll show, however, that far from proving them false, they actually proved nothing at all—except that a car *was* parked in the Gorsuch drive the night the deceased met his end, that it was of the same color, type, and make as the car Mrs. Gorsuch drove, such a car, I may add, as could have been had by rental from a dozen agencies here, none of which was checked by the police. The police say they tried this 'stunt,' as they call it, of driving up without lights on the stretch of road in question, and report 'it can't be done—anyone trying it would surely break his neck.' Well, that's what they think. But I'll bring a witness, your honor, who'll tell how it *was* done, a few nights before the fatal one, by a car which pulled up on him, also without lights, blew its horn at him as Miss Conlon says the horn was blown at Gorsuch—and forced him off the road. What with one thing and another, when Miss Conlon had told her story and been disbelieved by the police, he communicated with me instead of with them. He thinks, as Miss Conlon and the deceased were both at work in their nightclub the night this happened to him, that it was a practice run, preliminary to the real one, the one that caused Gorsuch's death—and I happen to think so too. Or in other words, your honor, the police did nothing at all to check the obvious possibility that Mrs. Gorsuch had a confederate, to whom she lent her car that night, and who——"

"Wait! Can you produce a confederate?"

"No, your honor. For some reason I can only conjecture, perhaps electrophobia, he hasn't come forward yet. He could exist, however. He could be sitting right now in this very courtroom. *Who are you looking at?*"

Mr. Pender ripped it at Sally, whose eyes had sought Clay's, and she at once ripped back: "*Who says I'm looking at anyone? What are you getting at? What are you trying to say?*"

"MR. PENDER!"

Judge Warfield's tone wasn't loud, but it filled the whole room. Obviously he was furious, and he went on: "I fine you one hundred dollars for contempt of this court."

"I apologize, your honor."

"I'll stand for no cheap, theatrical tricks of the kind you just indulged in, no booby-trapping of witnesses, no grandstand plays for the jury's benefit. You know better than that, Mr. Pender."

"I regret my outbreak, sir."

"It was not an outbreak. It was deliberate."

"I'm sorry. That I have to deny."

The judge was stern, but so was Mr. Pender. Taking out his wallet, he walked over to the bailiff and handed him a bill. "Have I permission to proceed?" he asked.

"As admonished, you have."

"Mrs. Gorsuch," he asked, "when I uttered the word 'confederate,' you looked at someone in the courtroom. May I ask who that person was?"

"That's better," said the judge.

"Well, Mr. Pender," said Sally, uncrossing and recrossing her very pretty legs, "I did look away, that's true, but what *at*, I disrecollect—not anything, that I recall. All it amounted to was: I was sick of looking at you."

The crowd laughed.

Judge Warfield laughed.

Mr. Kuhn laughed.
Mr. Pender laughed.

Clay's heart had skipped a beat when Sally's eyes drilled at him, and he had had a constricted sensation, as though he couldn't breathe. He had been feeling exultant while she was being clobbered, but now had a horrible suspicion that the clobbering was going too far, that it would soon get out of hand. At lunch he wanted to suggest that "we put the brakes on a little," but Mr. Pender wouldn't see him, being huddled at first with Mike Dominick and then with two other men. He ate at a table alone, and all through the afternoon was in a nervous sweat while Mr. Pender continued with Sally, scoring various points, mainly as he provoked her to a succession of ill-humored outbreaks, all sharply at variance with the wan, wilted widow she had seemed to be at first. But at last she was excused, and his spirits came up fast as Mr. Pender went grimly on, taking an insurance man over the jumps, as well as a city detective, who defended his work on the case, saying, "We deal with what is, not what might be, Mr. Pender—like his honor says, that could be anything, including snowballs in—wherever you're going next time." He was fairly sullen and made everyone laugh, including, once more, Mr. Pender. Clay was really bucked up when adjournment finally came, and his arm was caught going out as Mr. Pender whispered: "We got 'em on the run—it's really looking good. Hey, maybe it *was* the truth, what that dame said—Buster, I'm talking about. That would be something, wouldn't it? Me, believing my own case!"

Grace fed him and loved him and held his head to her breast, all the while murmuring encouragement: "What difference does it make who got clobbered today or how much? All that matters is Buster and getting her off. Once she's in the clear, we'll forget this dreadful mess, as we

202]

forget a dream. We've both done our share—and I'd like to remind you, Clay, twelve and a half thousand dollars aren't peanuts in anyone's court. We've done plenty already—I as well as you. And we'll continue that way—we'll do what has to be done to get this girl off. Once that's out of the way, the sun comes up once more!"

He was comforted and replied in amiable growls, suggesting around nine that "we call it off and go to bed." She agreed, and they got up from her modernist sofa, where they had been lying close, and started toward her bedroom. But before they reached it the buzzer sounded, and she went to open the door. Sally was in the hall, still in her black wool suit, her face twisted with rage. Coming in, she advanced on Clay and snarled at him: "You did that to me! You're in cahoots with that guy! I've seen you with him—don't pretend you had nothing to do with it! Well, let me tell you something. You——"

"Let me tell *you* something!"

Grace stepped in between and for a few moments told Sally off, for her "rotten, vindictive nature," which "left your father aghast, frightened Mr. El, froze poor Alec so he walked out on you, and finally brought you to this, the shadow of the electric chair! You—!"

With surprising dexterity for one so gracefully slim, she jerked Sally to her knees and began slapping her face. Sally screamed and cursed at her. At that, she really hooked things up. Holding Sally by the head, her hand clutching the soft felt hat, she slapped and slapped hard, so one of Sally's cheeks was suddenly red. Then: "Get up!" she snapped, stepping back. And when Sally rose: "Get out!"

"Go to hell, you poor mope. I'll go when I——"

Another slap cut that off, and then she grabbed Sally and hustled her to the door. Opening it, she pushed her out. But Sally, turning to Clay, snarled: "Not so fast. I still haven't told him what I came here to say! That shadow she's talking about, it's big enough for two. Try some more tricks, why don't you! *I'll not go alone!* Did you hear what I said?"

"We got 'em on the run. We must have or she wouldn't have come. If she's sweating blood, let her!"

23

But next morning Mr. Pender took a setback when the stuttering boy took the stand, the parking-lot attendant who had heard the brawl that night and told in exact detail how Buster had said: "I'll k-k-k-kill you!" He was not cross-examined, for the reason, as Mr. Pender explained at lunch: "I couldn't risk getting into the position of deriding a physical infirmity. Taking him over the jumps could easily have looked like that and only have made things worse. And, Clay, it's bad. That damned K-K-K-Katy stuff, 'I'll k-k-k-kill you,' is the kind of thing that stays in your ear when other stuff is forgotten—and it worries me. If it wasn't for that, this jury would vote an acquittal without even leaving the box—I could feel it yesterday that I had 'em. If *only* someone would come, would sit down at the table with us and whisper he heard that row, that he was out there parked in his car and could testify under oath that it didn't happen at all the way that clown said! A fat chance. All kinds of people have come—like that guy I'll put on the stand, the one who was run off the road, the one who'll shoot holes in the cops' report, and others, friends of Buster, offering to speak for her, be her character witness, believe it or not. But this one guy that I need won't show."

"Nat, he *has* showed," said Clay.

Startled, Nat stared, and Clay stared too, at his fingertips, as though a bit startled himself. "May surprise you, but I was parked out there myself, alongside the lot, and heard the whole thing. She was furious, but she didn't say she would kill him."

"Lean back, Clay, quick! I might kiss you!"

"Nevertheless, it's a fact."

"*But what were you doing there?*"

"Calling on Mike Dominick—I sell him meat, don't forget. After the row I decided it wasn't the night and drove home. Just the same, I was there."

"Brother! It's in the bag, we can't lose!"

And so it seemed, not only to Mr. Pender but also to Grace, when Clay called for a quick confab, from a courthouse pay station, just before court convened. "Oh, *certainly!*" she exclaimed. "If there's anything, anything at all, that you can truthfully say, to offset it, what that crazy boy said, by all means do it! Clay, the time is now, and the point of it is, *get her off!* Get her off, get her off, get her off! You're going to testify anyhow, and there's no sense at all in withholding the one thing that's going to count." So in midafternoon, when the state had finished its case, with a thick-faced electrician who told of the ladder incident, with Buster "bugging the guy, keeping at him to climb up and look"—so the threats on the parking lot was ominously prereinforced, redoubled in depth, so to speak—Clay took the stand to lead off for the defense, following a brief, solemn statement by Mr. Pender as to what his case would involve. Clay gave his name in his best big-shot manner: brisk, crisp, and importantly amiable. At once he hit a nice note of disbelief, of amused contempt, even, for the accusation against Buster, quickly disposing of the ladder incident. "For that I guess I'm responsible," he admitted in an easy, offhand way. Then, after telling of the visit from Mr. Alexis and Buster, the greetings from Mike, and so on, he said: "I warned Mr. Alexis—as he called himself to me—of the importance of getting his rails level, else his cradle, with Miss Conlon dangling from it, might go rolling off somewhere and land her behind the eight ball." He repeated the Mexico City anecdote, and Mr. Pender interrupted: "Did they test the rails at all?"

"They did. He, and later she."

"How did she test, Mr. Lockwood?"

"I lifted her, and she swung on them."

"How did he react to this?"

"He got sore that I should be touching her—he certainly didn't act like a guy that would ever desert her and—"

"Object," said Mr. Kuhn.

"Sustained," said the judge. And then to Clay: "Tell what he said or did, not what you think it meant."

"Yes, your honor," said Clay.

"The reporter will strike, the jury disregard, this last remark of the witness. Mr. Pender, please—?"

"What did he say when you lifted her?"

"That she should get down by herself—or something like that. I told him, not in my place—she might fall and break her leg, and Grant's, Inc., could be sued."

"And then?"

"I lifted her down."

"His manner, then, was jealous?"

"Object."

"Sustained."

So far Mr. Kuhn had shown no surprise, and he seemed aware already of what Clay related. But from the way he looked up, the next question obviously caught him off balance. "This visit," asked Mr. Pender, "did it have an aftermath?"

"It did, in a way," said Clay.

"Will you tell what it led to, then?"

"Well, there was Mike, who had sent his best regards by Alexis, and who I'd done nothing about all summer. But he buys my meat, after all, and I thought it was just about time for me to show some interest—in his reconditioned club and his plans for ten-ounce steaks."

"By interest, you mean you decided to call?"

"To drop in for a chat."

"At his club?"

"The Lilac Flamingo, that's right."

"And you did drop in?"

"I did—drove up there one night and parked."

"On the Lilac Flamingo lot?"

"On the street, next to the lot. Well, there was space there at the curb, and why waste a buck? On that parking attendant of Mike, who spatters spit when he talks—and I didn't have my umbrella."

"Object."

"Sustained."

Clay's crack got a laugh from the courtroom, but Mr. Pender didn't smile. "Mr. Lockwood," he said piously, "the boy can't help his affliction."

"He can help his l-l-l-lies," said Clay.

He sounded like Frank Fontaine, and this time the crowd gave a roar, with hand-clapping mixed in. Plainly they liked this big, good-looking witness, and their sudden silence was hostile as the judge said to Clay: "Mr. Lockwood, you've already been warned about gratuitous opinion. I fine you one hundred dollars for contempt."

Clay, patterning his behavior after Mr. Pender's, got up, took out his wallet, counted some bills, and handed them to the bailiff. But his face reddened, and before resuming his seat he said: "Your honor, if I showed contempt for this court, I did so unintentionally, and apologize. But, if this be contempt, to louse this silly case up by letting the truth in, I can only repeat: someone primed this little jerk up, filled him full of lies, as nothing took place that night resembling what he said here in this place today. I was there. I know. If I'm again in contempt, I have more cash in my pocket."

He sat down, and the judge thought a long time. Then, to Mr. Kuhn: "Are you going to move a mistrial?"

"Or a dismissal?" asked a grinning Mr. Pender.

". . . I'll let it ride," said Mr. Kuhn.

"Mr. Lockwood," said the judge, "this court is so impressed by your sincerity that I'm remitting your fine and instruct the bailiff to hand it back." Waiting until Clay had taken his money, he went on: "However, the law is the law, and if there's one more lapse on your part, cash will not be enough. I intend to send you to jail."

"Yes, your honor," whispered Clay.

"How long were you parked?" asked Mr. Pender.

"Only a few minutes—I meant to go in the club, but then Mr. Alexis came out, by a back door."

"In the dark you could recognize him?"

"Dark? The lot has floodlights on it."

"He was in costume, or what?"

"He was in dinner coat, black tie, and pink tarboosh, I believe it's called."

"Describe the tarboosh, please."

"Like a hat, in the form of a silk turban."

"You left the car then, or what?"

"I stayed where I was, beside my parked car—after my brush with him that day down at the shop I wanted no piece of this guy. I waited to see what he'd do, and sure enough he spoke to the boy, who trotted to a car and in the next minute or two backed it out in the middle."

"All right. Then what?"

"Miss Conlon piled out of the door."

"She was in costume, too?"

"She was in tights, trunks, and jacket."

"And what happened then, Mr. Lockwood?"

"They had this comedy brawl."

"Object."

"Sustained." The judge's manner was kind as he turned to Clay. "Tell what they said, tell what they did—omit your interpretation."

"He was laughing at her," snapped Clay at the judge, "and where I come from, that makes a comedy brawl. I tell it as well as I can. *Do you want the truth out of me or not?*"

"Objection withdrawn," said Mr. Kuhn.

"Tell it your way," said the judge.

"You tell it according to law," growled Mr. Pender at Clay. "I request the jury to disregard 'comedy brawl,' and pray the court to instruct the reporter to strike it."

"So ordered," said the judge.

"What did they say?" asked Mr. Pender.

"She said it was all a fake, what he had said to her about going home early to talk about divorce. She said: 'You're going back to her, that's what you're up to, you louse—so go on, see who gives a damn!' She screamed it, and he started to laugh. He said: 'So O.K., I'm lying, I'm the world's original louse—but come on, see for yourself! It'll cost us a million bucks, but anything to please!' And she said, 'Well, maybe I will,' and jumped in."

"Did she threaten to kill him at all?"

"No. At least, not that I heard."

"Did she make any threats of any kind?"

"Well—I guess she did, in a way. She said: 'O.K., go back to her, but don't you come back to me! You try coming back to me and see what happens to you!' "

"Did she say what she meant by that?"

"God knows what she meant. Maybe nothing."

By then it was nearly five, and when Mr. Kuhn, asked if he meant to cross-examine, said yes he certainly did, the judge adjourned until morning. Mr. Pender, leaving the courtroom, was exultant. "Boy, did you smash 'em up!" he whispered, grabbing Clay by the arm. "And with comical stuff yet! That 'l-l-l-lies' was worth all the rest put together!" He led Clay over to Buster, who was waiting for her policewoman, and she patted his arm, her eyes soft, her nervous fingers grateful. Home, he told it all to Grace, including his fine for contempt and its inexplicable remission. "It was remitted to you," she said, "because even that judge knew that you were telling the truth and that truth's day had come—it was entitled to be heard." They both laved themselves in the healing balm of the truth, it seemingly occurring to neither of them that the truth had not been told—that he had scarcely heard twenty words before leaving that night and that Mike had formed no part of his purpose. But, in their twisted, left-handed way, they had helped basic justice, and so were warmed for one night.

"Mr. Lockwood, where did you dine the night in whose early morning hours you drove to the Lilac Flamingo?"

". . . Well, I don't just offhand recall. I generally dine at the Channel City Yacht Club and no doubt did that night."

"Alone?"

"I do as a rule, Mr. Kuhn."

"And then you went home?"

"I assume so, yes."

"You drove?"

"I always do."

"In your own car?"

"Of course."

"What did you do with it then?"

"Just a moment, please."

Mr. Pender got to his feet, saying: "Your honor, I don't like to clog up a trial with objections that merely obstruct, but I must say I don't see the point of all this. We'll stipulate the car if it makes any difference, and it's assumed, I would think, that Mr. Lockwood did *something* with it—after all, it won't go in his pocket. So unless there's some reason for this I don't see, I must object at this point."

"So."

Mr. Kuhn was very quiet and then went on: "Perhaps it's just as well, your honor, that counsel has raised the question, but before I answer, I suggest that the court exclude the jury."

"Very well."

Waiting until the bailiff had shoed the jury out, Mr. Kuhn went on, still in his quiet way. And he had hardly said ten words when Clay's head began to reel, for he knew his perfect alibi was rising up to destroy him. "What he did with his car," said Mr. Kuhn, "what he did with his night, these commonplaces which my colleague would have me assume, are actually of the essence, for they prove that Mr. Lockwood, in spite of his outbreak yesterday, his noisy appeal to Truth, was actually lying out of hand in all that he told this court, of his trip to the club that night, the reasons he had for taking it, what he heard, and what he saw. I'll bring incontrovertible evidence that he spent the night at home, that he never left his apartment, that his story was pure invention. In fact, so overwhelming is this evidence that I intend to charge him with perjury and ask that he be held, when he leaves the witness stand, for the action of the grand jury."

He produced a paper, approached the judge's desk, and, when Mr. Pender had joined him, let him read. Then, in a low tone, he went on: "Your honor, when that insurance came to light, when Mrs. Gorsuch rang in about it, the police checked this girl out—the defendant, Miss Conlon, especially the men she'd been seeing. There were four, including this man Lockwood, who had been the subject of a thinly veiled newspaper item, which coupled him with the defendant. What he did the night of the crime was thoroughly investigated, and so far as complicity went, he was cleared one hundred percent. And in fact, until he took the stand yesterday, he hadn't figured in this case. Now, however——"

"Your honor," asked Mr. Pender, "what is this, anyway? Here's a man, a community leader, president-elect of one of our biggest corporations, who takes the stand for a girl he thinks falsely accused, and his reward, on the basis of still another police report, is to be charged in this court with perjury without any——"

"Yes, Mr. Kuhn," said the judge. "I'm disturbed."

"Then I hold the charge at this time."

"Perjury is easy to allege when a witness won't say what we want him to. And here, it seems to me, you're less concerned with a violation of the law as such than with winning this other case—or in other words, you seem to be using it tactically, as a means of smoking this witness out, as the saying goes. That I can't have."

"If so, I wasn't aware of it."

"Of course if the cross-examining develops evidence of a substantial kind, the court itself must take cognizance of it."

"Then I await your honor's decision."

"Bailiff, bring in the jury."

Mr. Kuhn then began his dreadful drumfire, and Clay could feel himself sweat. He brought out the visit to the garage, the arrangements about the car; Clay's parking it outside, snug to the curb on Spring Street; his little scene with Doris, and her putting the keys in his box; his arrival in the apartment, his call to Pat, his call to Miss Helm, and her call to Atlantic City. "And then?" asked Mr. Kuhn.

"She called me to check on the rate."

"And you told her?"

"That forty a day was all right."

"And then?"

"I started to take off my clothes, but was restless and didn't feel like going to bed. Then I remembered Mike, and he seemed as good an excuse as any to get out of the house again and go somewhere. So I went."

"Out through the lobby, of course?"

"No—after all that hocus-pocus about putting the keys in the box, I would have felt kind of silly asking Doris to start over again. So I dropped duplicate keys in my pocket and went out the back way. I keep three or four sets around, ignition keys and trunk keys, on little spiral rings." He took out a pair and clinked them at Mr. Kuhn. "I took a set from a bureau drawer and drove off without telling Doris."

"Straight to the Lilac Flamingo?"

"That's right—to the side street by the club."

"When was this?"

"At a guess, I'd say I left at eleven-thirty."

"And then you came back?"

"I did."

"Parking where?"

"Same place as before."

"The same way as before? Snug? To the curb?"

"Mr. Kuhn, I haven't the faintest idea. I always park according to law, or try to—and in this case I suppose I followed habit. But if independent recollection is what you want, I don't have any."

"What time was this?"

"One-thirty, one-forty-five."

214]

"And you went in the back way, as before?"

"No, I went in through the lobby."

"Being checked in? By the late man? On the desk?"

"No—Frank was asleep."

So far, having had his moment of warning, while the lawyers wrangled, Clay had made lightning improvisations, and feeling they might be believed, had regained his big-shot manner, a combination of cold civility and slightly annoyed impatience. But it all began to wear thin when Mr. Kuhn abruptly asked: "Isn't it true, Mr. Lockwood, that you stayed home that night, that you didn't leave at all, by the front door, back door, or any door, and that you've told this incredible tale simply to help Miss Conlon—that you've been her paramour and are trying to get her off, at any cost, even a breach of the truth?"

"No, Mr. Kuhn, it's not true."

"You've been a visitor at her home?"

"I've never been to her home."

"Mr. Kuhn picked up his report and, elaborately letting the jury see, asked Clay: "You deny that on August eighteenth last you went to her home, leaving around dusk?"

"Her apartment house, not her home."

"Explain this distinction, please."

Clay's mouth, disconnected from his mind, began to talk, explaining his concern for Buster, her safety in the projected act, and "I wanted to check on it, what had been done with the rails—and I wanted no piece of Gorsuch, or Alexis, as he called himself with me. So, being in Baltimore one evening, I decided to look her up, and after finding her in the phone book drove over to that part of town. I located her place, went in, and checked the mailboxes, lighting a match to look, as I'm sure your report says. Her box was there, but then I decided I'd better call, rather than barge out of the blue. So I went up the street, looking for a call box, and, not finding any, came back. Then, to my surprise, she came bouncing out of the doorway and down the steps. So we had our talk, right there on the sidewalk, and I found everything had been done in the way I had said it should be. But then we went on to other things and stepped into a vestibule—of an office building nearby. You want the details of what we said?"

"Not particularly," said Mr. Kuhn.

"WHY DON'T YOU WANT THE DETAILS?" thundered Clay.

His mouth having come up with a tale that at least steadied his nerves, he summoned courage to take the offensive, and sounded once more, as he had the day before, like the big, overbearing, self-righteous business executive, determined to be heard. "Or do you only want part of the truth? The part that'll burn this girl."

"Then—the details," said Mr. Kuhn.

Clay told of Buster's concern over Mr. Alexis, that he was 'giving me the air, so he can go back to *her*—out of gratitude for what she did, helping his father die, at least as he thought, and bringing him all that money.' Pointing at Sally, whose eyes looked like fragments of glass, Clay explained: "She meant that lady there, Mrs. Sally Gorsuch—though of course, Mr. Kuhn, your police reports cover it. I hope you've referred to them—I know of course you wouldn't suppress anything."

"Mr. Lockwood, you've been warned," snapped the judge.

"If you're trying to shut me up, I won't shut!"

Clay looked at Judge Warfield, as utter recklessness swept caution aside. It was his great moment at the trial, and for a long interval silence hung on the courtroom. Then Mr. Kuhn resumed: "So even then, on August eighteenth, the defendant, Miss Conlon, had her mind on revenge?"

"On a replacement, I'd say," Clay told him.

" . . . Replacement? What do you mean?"

"Some guy—in Alexis' place."

"Ah! Meaning you?"

"Yeah! We kidded along about it!"

"And you kissed her?"

"You bet I did. She kisses nice."

24

Mr. Kuhn had no further questions, Mr. Pender only a few deferential ones of a kind to remind the jury of Clay's personal eminence, and there was no more mention of perjury. Nevertheless, Clay's face was drawn as he left the stand, and he didn't look at the judge, the jury, or anyone, not even at Buster, where she sat trying to beam him a smile. Not waiting for lunch with Mr. Pender, he hurried out to his car and drove home, finding nobody there. He went to Grace's bedroom and flung himself down on her bed, a square, newfangled thing with shelves in the place of a headboard and no footboard at all. There, some time later, returning from market, she popped in and sat down beside him. But when she asked how it went, he merely said, "O.K., I guess," in a vague, dull way, still keeping his face in the pillow. But when she opened the paper she had bought, he turned over and stared at the headline. It was *The Pilot's* noon edition, which had the perjury charge but not its subsequent withdrawal. In a jerky, dramatic way then, he said: "So—you want to know how it went, that's how. They later withdrew the charge—but the word was used—and for a couple of minutes there, to leave that court I'd have had to put up bail."

"But *how* could they charge you with that?"

"I was guilty of it, that's how."

"But you never lied in your life. Not once!"

"And I didn't lie now—that's where it gets good. But down underneath the fraction of truth I was telling, the whole truth was rumbling around, and they heard it! They didn't buy what I said, especially not that jury. They knew something was wrong, even if they didn't know what. And that Kuhn even came out and said it, that I lied under oath—and the cockeyed part was that the lying he thought I had done, I didn't do, at all. . . . Ah, why slice it so thin? I blew it, that's all."

"But how could you? Yesterday——"

"Oh, boy, yesterday! You should have heard me today!"

"Clay, will you calm down? What happened?"

"My alibi, remember? It ruined me."

"But—it was supposed to be good."

"And was, airtight, lawyer-proof, and copper-riveted, and that was the trouble with it. It exploded right in my face. Hoist by my own petard. What is a petard, if you know?"

"Why—a powder keg, I think."

"And how! *And how!*"

Disconnectedly, half-heartedly, he tried then to tell her what had happened, and did sketch out most of it. But then he broke off, pleading: "Don't ask me to talk, Grace. If I had scored, I'd say so, don't worry—no one's as gabby as I am when I've stuff to brag about. The very fact I don't *want* to tell it is the proof that there's nothing to tell—at least, that you'd want to hear. And the worst of it is, I hurt the girl's case instead of helping it."

"Well, that, at least, I can bear."

Her waspish tone caught his ear, and he pressed her to know what she meant. "I mean, it serves her right," she told him virtuously.

"In what way serves her right?"

"Well, Clay! Look at what she did!"

"And what did she do, Grace?"

220]

"Well! The life that she led with Alec!"

"She did no more with him than I did with Alec's wife. And if that's what serves her right, all I can say is——"

"*And* trying to put it on Sally!"

"Grace, Sally did it!"

"But Sally was not even there!"

"Sally was in it up to the hilt. She planned it with me—she's guilty, just as guilty as I am."

"And I am, don't forget!"

" . . . And let's have an end of *that!*"

He stared at the ceiling, went on: "Your wanting to share with me, your standing by me the way you have, is the one bright spot in this mess. But don't let's play games. No one's here with us but God, and I don't think we're kidding Him. So let's not kid ourselves. You share my pain, I know—and that warms me, fills me with hope, and gives me strength. You can't share my guilt. Nobody can except—"

"My daughter?"

"Yes."

He pulled her to him, unbuttoned her sweater, broke the strap of her bra, and nuzzled and kissed and inhaled.

That went on for three days, with interruptions only for the meals she cooked and brought him, and for her hourly trips outside, to buy papers as they came out. He took little interest, however, as she read him the rest of the testimony, Buster's outbreak on the stand, arguments by the lawyers, and speculation as to the verdict while the jury was "out." And his face was blank as she came in the fourth day, tossed him a paper, and said: "Well, it's over—they convicted her. Of manslaughter, whatever that is. Less than murder apparently. So, she won't go to the chair. So, you did what you could. So, do you mind? If we forget this dreadful girl? And talk about something else?"

"Forget her?" he said dully. "How could I?"

"Well, you'd better! She's all but ruined your life!"

He glanced through the paper, learning that Mr. Pender had moved for a new trial and had served notice that, failing that, he would appeal, and that sentence would be passed on Monday. Then, almost as though in a stupor, he asked: "And why should I forget her? Or even try to forget her?"

"She has it coming, that's why!"

"Has what coming, Grace?"

"*This!* If she'd lived a decent life, if she'd let Alec alone, above all, if she hadn't jumped in that car, just to plague him and act like a hussy, none of this would have happened—to say nothing of that other, the lie she told the police about seeing Sally's car! Oh, yes! These chickens come home to roost! She has no one to thank but herself!"

"*She has no one to thank but me—and Sally.*"

"Is there something between you and this girl?"

He didn't answer, but got up in robe and pajamas, went into the bathroom, and shaved, bathed, and combed. When he came out the bed was made and his clothes were lying on it, his suit, underwear, and shirt, with three neckties to choose from; his shoes and stockings on the floor. Biting his lip, he dressed, then went to the living room, where she sat in her knitted suit, primly waiting. "Well?" she asked. "Is there? It said in the paper you kissed her and that 'She kisses nice.'"

"She does—and there's nothing between us."

"Maybe not, but I'm sick of her just the same."

"Grace, she's convicted of something I did."

"Oh, but there's more to it than that!"

"There's no more to it than that."

"Oh, yes! Don't forget! *I* did something *too!*"

"*Grace! For God's sake, knock it off!*"

She bounced up, as though on springs, at the crackle of his voice, and was rigid as his arms went around her and he began to talk in her ear: "Honey, what you did I'll never

222]

forget—the money was just the beginning—your wanting to share—your standing by me like a rock—to me are nine-hundred-percent magnificent—looking at you, where *you* sit. But *I* don't sit where you sit—the place where I sit is different. I'm guilty, you're not. What you've done proves you love me, as God knows I love you." He held her close and kissed her, then kissed her again and again, until she began to kiss back. Then, releasing her, he walked away until he faced the wrap-closet door. "But that's all it proves," he whispered.

Opening the closet, he took out his coat and hat and put them on. "Where are you going?" she asked.

"Out. In the park. Think."

"You mean, you prefer to be alone?"

"I sit alone, I must think alone."

But he didn't stay in the park, beyond marching around a few minutes, to go through the visible motions in case he was being watched. When some bushes screened him from sight, he quickened his pace abruptly and walked to the Marlborough, letting himself in the back way. On entering the apartment, he drew a deep breath, as he did on entering a cold room, but for a different reason. Instead of testing, he was savoring: the familiar, deeply loved smell of a place that was neat as a pin, and yet lived in, warm, fragrant, and his own. He glanced at his pictures, then took off his things and went back to the "office," removing the typewriter cover, sitting down, and settling himself to work. He didn't type well, but he typed well enough, and now began to tap out the dreadful tale of his downfall. He wrote in sextuplicate, using sets Miss Helm had got him, of six sheets each with carbons between, with double spacing and ample margins, in case pen corrections would be necessary. He began at the beginning, telling his meeting with Sally, his suspicions of what she intended, her crime down at the beach, and his offer to do what she wanted. He told of the rehearsals on the road, his pouring of paint markers, "which should still show on the shoulder, susceptible of ready check"; of what happened that terrible night, of Buster's scream, of the hubcap and what he had done with it, "another thing susceptible of check, and it's still down in the slough." He wound up: "I put on my lights just as Miss Conlon said, on the stand and to the police, and it all happened just as she said except for the license number, on which her instinct colored her vision— not saying her instinct was wrong." He then typed a form of affidavit, swearing "the foregoing is true," and under this typed:

Copies to:
Hon. Leonard Warfield, Judge of the Superior Court.
Hon. John Kuhn, state's attorney, Chinquapin County.
Hon. John Pender, Law Building, Channel City, Md.
Mrs. Alexander Gorsuch, the Chinquapin-Plaza Hotel.
Mrs. Clay Lockwood, Rosemary Apartments, Channel City, Md.

Around four he interrupted to call Miss Sophie Henning, who ran a small, one-room secretarial bureau down on the second floor, and who was a notary public, asking her to stand by for a visit around 5:30. He used her outside phone, looking her up in the book, instead of the inside phone, so as not to alert Miss Homan that he was in the apartment. He had scarcely hung up when his own outside phone rang, and he hesitated about answering. He decided not to and let it ring on while he went back to his typing, finishing up the statement and the envelopes he would need to send his copies out. He was careful with the addresses and with the stamps, but he left them open after putting the statements in. Then he sat down again and typed up a brief will, leaving all that he had to Grace, and putting it in her envelope. Then he penned her a brief note, telling her that he loved her, and put it in too.

He used the freight car to go down to Miss Henning's, finding her a neat little gray-haired woman in a pink embroidered smock. She didn't look at his statement, but got out her notary stamp, clamped it on all six copies, and penned her signature in after smilingly asking him to raise his hand and swear. But when she came to the will, she said: "Oh, that takes two witnesses, Mr. Lockwood. If you'd written it longhand, holograph, I mean, it wouldn't take any at all, but typed up it needs two other persons to sign." She called a girl, an extra typist she had, and with her signed the will. Clay, after paying the fifty-cent notary fee for each of the six statements, and the one-dollar witness fees for the will, passed out his usual five-dollar bills, murmured his thanks, and left, sealing his envelopes and tucking them into his pocket.

He walked the one flight down, using the back stairs again, stood on Kennedy Drive, caught a cab, and drove to the Chinquapin-Plaza. At the room clerk's window a strange girl gave him Sally's suite numbers, 1942A, 1942B, and 1942C. "But when you call," she admonished him, "be sure and ask for 1942A, or there'll be a mix-up. B is the nursery and C the maid's room, and ringing the phone in those rooms just causes running around." He didn't call, though the house phones were just a few steps away. Instead, he went to the flower shop and asked for lilies, "you know, like Easter." Since it wasn't Easter, the clerk seemed puzzled, saying: "Well—we do keep some in stock, for funerals mostly. But we usually make them up in wreaths or blankets or basket. If that's what you have in mind—?" Clay said: "Something simple—you know, like a bunch, with a ribbon tied around." The clerk then concluded he wanted them to "put on a grave," and Clay, rather quickly, said: "Yeah, that's it. That's the idea, of course." Presently the girl

[225

brought them, tied up with a white satin ribbon, and Clay nodded as he sniffed their necrotic smell. She did them up in a box, a white one with another white satin ribbon. He paid, went out in the lobby again, and entered the express elevator. "Nineteen," he told the operator, who pressed a button that lit a red light in a panel.

25

"*Hey, stupid, couldn't you listen just once to your wife? She's not so dumb, and she's not even going to respect it, this grand caper of yours that you're getting ready to cut. Listen: Suppose the girl was convicted, who says she'll stay that way? Nat may get her off. And even if he doesn't, manslaughter isn't so bad—a year in jail, if that. Wake up, get with it, what's waiting for you now! A beautiful woman that loves you, a job to dream about, money, position, probably kids pretty soon, everything! Don't throw it away by this stunt! All you need do is nothing, and you're sitting on top of the world!*"

Clay's lips were moving as he stepped from the car, and when the door had banged behind him he stood for some moments alone in front of the mail chute, his eyes closed, his mouth still making a mumble. Then his teeth clenched and he took out the envelopes, shuffling them onto the box as he checked all the addresses. The one addressed to Sally he put back in his pocket. The others, one by one, he slipped into the chute. When the last one had gone flashing down the glass, he turned and walked down a corridor, peering at the numbers on the doors. Reaching a small entrance hall, he saw Sally's number beside it. Stepping in, he touched the buzzer of 1942A. A maid opened, a pretty girl in black uniform, white apron, cuffs, and cap. When Clay asked for

"Mrs. Alexis," she made him knicks, and said, with a Swedish accent, she would "see if madame is in."

Then Sally appeared, in plain black wool dress. "Oh, Clay!" she said, as though not much surprised. "Come in." Then, to the maid: "Will you take charge of him now? When he's ready for bed, bring him in to be kissed good night." Then, laughing up at Clay, in red rompers suit, with gray eyes exactly like Grace's, a little boy appeared and stood touching his mother. The maid took him into 1942B. Motioning Clay inside, Sally noticed the box, said: "If those are Mother's flowers, she's on her way up. She's been looking all over for you—there's been some sort of call from Mankato."

"Yeah—I'm fired, no doubt."

"No—you're president *now*, it seems. Mr. Svenson, if that's the name, has had a stroke or something—and you're to report right away— No, I'm not spoiling Mother's surprise— she told me to tell you, *begged* me to tell you, as soon as you came, if you came!"

"What made her think I would come? Did she say?"

"Well, she doesn't know *where* you are!"

When she said, "Take off your things," he put his hat and coat on a chair, the flowers on a table, then looked stunned when she said: "Pity about Buster, isn't it? I mean, that she got off so light. But at least it'll teach her a lesson."

" . . . Yeah? What lesson is that?"

"That crime doesn't pay—like slander."

"Against you, for instance?"

"That's it, Clay. It annoys me."

"Could be a point, at that."

Their tone, though he still looked incredulous, was airy to the point of vacuity, and she was utterly casual as she asked: "But before Mother gets here, was there something you wanted of me?"

"Yes—this. I thought you should see it."

He got her envelope out, going through a long rigmarole

228]

of apology, that it was sealed and addressed for the mails. "Protocol," he smiled, "you know, that stuff that you taught in the charm school, says it ought to be open, with 'By hand' typed on, or 'Kindness of Clay Lockwood,' or something of that sort. But I sealed it by mistake and stamped it before I realized. I hope you'll overlook it. Here, I'll open it for you—"

"It's quite all right. I can do it."

Now sitting on the big sofa of this brocade and satin suite, she took a paper cutter from the low table in front of her and slit the envelope's flap. Then she took out the statement and started to read. Then, jumping up, she snarled: "What is this, Clay? A joke?"

"No! It tells what happened, that's all."

She tried to read on, but couldn't. She skipped to the second page, to the third, fourth, and last. There she saw the notary seal, the signature, and those listed for copies. "But Clay," she quavered, her mouth covered with spittle, "don't you know what this can mean?"

"Why, sure—it'll get the thing out in the open. That's what it says: 'To Whom It May Concern.' It means everyone—the whole wide world and its brother-in-law."

"You'd better damned well not mail it!"

"I did mail it."

"You—? But it could mean the electric chair! For both of us. Were you insane? For you! For me!"

"It could, but fortunately it won't."

"What do you mean, it won't?"

"Open your flowers. They're for you, not Grace."

He got up and brought her the box, and with jerky fingers, her eyes still searching his face, she worked the ribbon off and got the top off the box. " . . . Why," she exclaimed, "they're funeral lilies!"

"That's right, and the funeral is now."

Still searching his face, she saw eyes that met hers with the

[229

unseeing stare of a corpse. She drew breath to scream, but he seemed ready for that. His hand was at her throat, his thumb on her larynx, pressing it down. As she struggled she slipped to the floor, but he didn't relax his grip. When she was dead, he lifted her to the sofa again, closing her bulging eyes and smoothing down her dress. From a table he took a bright tapestry scarf, a thing four to five feet long and twelve inches or so wide. He spread it over her, to cover face, body, and legs. Then he folded her hands over it, put the lilies on her chest. Then, putting ribbon, paper, etc., back in the box and pressing the top on, he dropped it into a wastebasket and sat down in a chair to wait.

After an eternity the buzzer sounded, and when he opened the maid was there, the little boy in her arms, both faces aglow with expectancy. "Ah—could you give us a few minutes more?" he said with a death's-head smile. "We're not quite finished yet—we'll let you know." The maid, looking baffled, said: "So, good, ja," and took her burden back to 1942B. He had barely returned to the chair when the phone rang, but in another room. Sure it was Grace, he felt he had to answer and opened a door across from the sofa. It was the bedroom, and on the night table the phone was ringing, but a man sat on the bed, whom Clay had never seen—in bathrobe and slippers, his face turned toward the door, as though expecting Sally to answer. He stiffened, but Clay paid no attention, striding past him and answering the phone. "Clay?" said Grace. "At last!" He told her to "come on up, and get a move on." Then he went back to the sitting room, closing the door after him without speaking to the man or the man's speaking to him. He opened the outer door and stood in the entrance hall waiting for Grace. In a minute or two she came, and inanely he said: "Hello."
"Clay!" she said, kissing him. "Thank God!"
"Yeah?" he said dully. "For what?"

"Finding you, for one thing! But that's not all. Darling, I'm bursting with news! Pat called, he'd been trying to reach you all day, and finally the office remembered me and put him through. He wants you out there right away. Mr. Svenson has had a stroke, and you're to take over at once. There's more, but—I'll tell you about it later. I'd no sooner talked to him than I called that man Nat Pender, and when I agreed to foot the bill, two hundred and fifty dollars, he said he could get her out—that Buster—on bail! I went over at once with my check, to his office, and there she was, out! I met her, there by his desk. Darling, if you could kiss her, you do have a strong stomach—that's all that I say about *that*. But there's still more! By finagling the appeal somehow—by hinting he may not file one if her sentence is not too severe—he thinks the judge will be tempted to suspend it so she goes free. *So!* It was much ado about nothing! She's practically in the clear! *Now* what do you think of your Little-Miss-Fix-It—me?"

"I'm proud of you, as always."

"Kiss me."

He kissed her. Then: "She'll be quite clear tomorrow."

" . . . Quite clear? How?"

"I've confessed. . . . Mailed a sworn statement to the judge and everyone. Booted the beans into the fire—told the truth at last."

"Oh, Clay—*no!*"

"Yes."

"Clay, she's not worth saving! You are!"

"She's a human being."

"Not too damned human, though. My, what a cheap, horrible trollop! It means nothing to her at all—she was there cracking jokes, anything for a laugh, she kept saying. And making passes at Pender—successfully: he means to take her! And I say he could pay for her bail!"

"Then, stop payment on your check."

" . . . Clay, what do we do now?"

"We don't do anything. From here on out, it's you. Grace, listen to me now: this child, little Elly, is going to be brought in to kiss Sally good night. It mustn't happen. You must see to that."

"But, Clay, she's his mother!"

" . . . Was. She's dead."

"God have mercy, what have you done?"

"I've killed her. But there's more, Grace."

" . . . What?"

"The ugliest thing came to light after—after it happened. There's a man there in her bed, in bathrobe, slippers, and not much else that I saw. Waiting for her, apparently. He means nothing to me and, I imagine, less than that to you. Nevertheless, you must see that he's cleared of this crime. You must——"

"I can't take any more! I can't! *I can't!*"

She reeled against the doorjamb, and he caught her, holding her close, murmuring into her ear, kissing her. The door of 1942B opened on a crack and, after an eye peeped out, closed again. Regaining her strength a little, she asked: "Why can't you see that he's cleared?"

"I have something else to do."

Her eyes showed that she knew what he meant, and once more they stared at each other as though across bellowing chasms. She whispered: "Then—I'll see—that he's cleared—I'll see—to everything."

"Will you kiss me?"

Grandeur touched her as she gave him this last seal of devotion, warmly, compassionately, comprehendingly, then turned and entered the suite.

He was halfway up the corridor before he realized he had forgotten his coat as well as his hat, but dourly observed: "Where you're going you won't need them—either one." He pulled open the glass door beside the mail chute and began stumbling up slick metal stairs. There were several flights, and he was out of breath when he came to the top and pushed open an iron door. Then he stepped out on top of the world, into the jumble of chimneys and ventilators and fire-escape tops and TV antennae and sunbathers' recliners that clutters a hotel roof. It was a crisp, clear autumn night, with the stars above all aglitter, and the lights below all ashimmer, in red, yellow, green, orange, and blue. For some moments he paused to look. And then this man who had done so much, who loved applause so well, who never took no for an answer and had only now tasted defeat, mumbled incoherences heard only by God and strode to the parapet. After a glance at the ground, to make sure no one was there, he vaulted and went hurtling down on the parking lot, twenty-two stories below. In 1942A, half an hour later or so, a woman of stone sat while police, press, and hotel men milled around, a terrified child in her lap, a sobbing maid at her feet, and answered the dreadful questions a detective kept putting to her. They concerned what was there on the sofa, and "that body we found on the ramp," as well as the cowering figure, in bathrobe and nightshirt and slippers, who stood in the bedroom door and pleaded for leave to dress. At last, though, it was over, and the detective said "O.K." to the stretcher bearers, "O.K." to the cowering man, and "O.K., thanks, ma'am, you been great," to her. Then Grace, the child held close, the maid following behind with clothing, blankets, toys, and a mammoth teddy bear, went stalking exaltedly out, into the night, into the world, into what was left of her life.